CW01459947

Lover Boy

The Boys of Apartment 13 Book 2

Brianna Flores

Copyright © 2024 Brianna Vega

All rights reserved

ISBN: 9798340757265

The characters and events portrayed in this book are fictitious. Any similarity to real persons, living or dead, is coincidental and not intended by the author.

No part of this book may be reproduced, or stored in a retrieval system, or transmitted in any form or by any means, electronic, mechanical, photocopying, recording, or otherwise, without express written permission of the publisher.

Cover design by: Brianna Vega

To the readers who wished Liam had picked Cade.
Those two are kindred spirits and not at all right
for each other. Here's 70k words to prove it.

Contents

Content Warning

This book does contain topics that may be triggering to some readers. This list may contain spoilers and I do recommend skipping it if you'd like to avoid those. However, if you do have triggers and/or just want to know what sorts of naughty fun you can look forward to, please read below.

A consensual sexual relationship between stepbrothers (pseudoincest)

Two pigheaded boys who like to fight as much as they like to fuck

Sadomasochism

Consensual Non-Consent (CNC)

Degradation in the form of derogatory language

Depictions of self-harm and scarring (off-page)

Depictions of chronic pain

Depictions of depression and anxiety

*Negative thoughts and feelings
involving insecurities*

*Misuse of prescription medication prescribed
to help alleviate anxiety and depression*

Spit - that's all I'll say about that one

One scene depicting primal play

Safeword usage

Minimal use of proper anal sex preparation

Detailed sex involving two men

Feelings of hate between the MCs

Mentions of a miscarriage (off page)

Death of a parent (by suicide, off page)

Author's Note

Howdy pals!

If you were one of the amazing people who put up with my shitty health and pushing of this release date, thank you! Seriously, thank you so much. I would have fully understood if you'd lost all interest, but you being here means so much!

The themes in this book are heavier than those in Pretty Boy, and because of that I do want to add a warning outside of the content warning: My boys either like feeling pain or causing pain and I know not everyone likes to read those things. It's a pretty prevalent feature in this story, so keep that in mind.

I really wanted to emphasize just how wrong for Cade his best friend is, so while there are a lot of similarities between Lover Boy and Pretty Boy, this book is it's own creation.

Lover Boy is moderately angsty and I so hope you enjoy it!

Happy reading!

-*Brianna Flores*

Prologue

Nic

Five years ago...

"**M**om?"

Instead of an answer, all I get is a sickening feeling in the pit of my stomach.

"Mom, I have to go," I try again, this time taking a step into the darkened room. I make sure to tell her that I *have* to go—that I emphasize how it's not my choice to leave her.

For what feels like the hundredth time just today, I think of my dad and feel disgusted by him.

"Mom..." I swallow back the plea, the words I know she won't really hear.

When my throat starts to burn, I straighten my spine and step back. She doesn't need the burden of my emotions. She's dealing with enough of her own. So, I settle on just finishing the goodbye.

"I love you. I'll see you in a few days, okay? I'll call

you. Try to answer it..." I look at her bedside table to make sure her phone is plugged in. I don't want it to die. "There's food in the freezer." No answer, no reassurance that she'll bother to actually get up and eat anything. Paulina, our next-door neighbor, has said that she'll come over once a day, and while asking for help makes me sick, it is a relief.

She'll make sure she eats something. And a demented part of me thinks that she'll be here if my mom...

I shouldn't even be leaving. She needs me here. My dad doesn't understand. He makes me leave her because he doesn't know how bad things have gotten, what kinds of damage he's done. Probably doesn't even care.

I still don't know if I'm doing the right thing by keeping quiet. But then I think of telling him, the only other person I really know who's supposed to help me, and I just know it wouldn't be good. They'd take me away—I'm only sixteen. I just have to suck it up, wait a couple more years.

But god. I'm so tired.

"Okay, Mom." I sigh. "I'll be home soon."

She doesn't move. She stays there, a lifeless lump under her covers in her dark room, and just doesn't move.

I can hear him honking as I enter the living room, and it dissolves any sorrow I was feeling. Something ugly and visceral takes its place, something hard and sharp. Something easier. I fucking hate him. And I hate them just as much. My stepmother and her son.

I know that it's my dad's fault, and I shouldn't blame them, the family he tries so hard to force on me. *He* was the one who had an obligation to my mom. But she knew he was married. It takes a shitty person to break up a family like that, to just take someone's husband and someone's father away. And Cade... he just pisses me off.

I don't even want my dad anymore, but it still bothers me that Cade gets him every single day. That he gets to see the parts of him that aren't absolute shit. That he gets to see my dad make *his* mom happy.

I used to get that. Now, I'm forced to see what's left —the after. After he's broken her.

He honks the horn again—holds it for an obnoxiously long time, and my hand stalls on the door handle. I don't feel all that well, but I don't know if it's a cold or the feeling of dread leaving typically causes. But I'm both cold and hot, so tired as I stand here in misery—the front door is all that's keeping me from seeing them. My dad's new, better family.

I drag in a heavy breath, sucking it up as I wipe a bead of sweat off my forehead before finally pulling the door open. My dad is smiling, but I'm not sure why.

Maybe because he's won. I'm old enough that I should be able to decide which parent I want to spend time with, but he's threatened more than once to take my mom to court if I don't go with him, and I know she couldn't handle that. She probably wouldn't even show.

And so here I am, walking towards him and feeling my blood thicken into something solid, something weighing me down more and more with every step I take. It's hard to breathe. It's always hard to breathe, like my lungs are operating on manual and if I don't make the conscious choice to do it, I just won't.

I have to look away from his face, not wanting to let him see just how repulsed I am by this whole situation. It's been three years of this, and it hasn't gotten any easier. Not for me and definitely not for my mom.

"Mijo, help him with his bags."

It confuses me for a split second before I realize he's talking to Cade. My hands tighten on the straps of my bags as he rushes to listen, to be the dutiful *son* my dad has always wanted.

"I got it, little brother," I say with a bite, using the words my father used when he introduced us to each other.

He scoffs, his stupid smile that seems to always be there in the presence of my dad disappearing, but I ignore him. It's just two bags and I'm more than capable of throwing them in the trunk myself.

"Your hair..." It's Tracey who speaks when I get in the car. "The white patch is growing. Isn't it, Anton? Doesn't it look bigger?" She turns around in her seat to look at me, and I do my best not to look daggers at her. I'll snap soon, but avoiding a fight for as long as I can is for the best.

A lot of people get fixated on my skin and what the vitiligo does to my hair, and she's no exception. She brings it up every time I see her. Every. Time. I have two patches of white hair on my head, one just at my hairline for everyone to see the split second they look at me, and the other on the back of my head—and nobody lets me forget it.

Her hand reaches out like she's going to touch me, and I recoil. I can't help it, but what the hell? What about my demeanor made her think I'd just let her, of all people, touch me like that?

"Sorry!" She holds her palm out like she just approached a skittish dog or something and it just bothers me that much more.

"Nic," my dad's voice warns. "Don't start."

My mouth opens to say something, but nothing comes out. He doesn't care, doesn't want to hear it.

"Wipe that look off your face," he tells me, but since I can't do that just yet, I turn my head and face the window.

"It was my fault." Tracey's voice is small, gnaws at me in a way that itches. *She's so fucking fake.* They all are.

"She didn't even do anything," Cade defends his mom, and I don't bother keeping the dirty look off of my face as I look at him. He's expressed more than once that he doesn't like how I treat his mom, but I don't care. He doesn't even know the half of it.

He just smiles all the damn time as he lives his happy life with his happy mom and *my* dad. So fuck him.

My dad tries to change the subject. He lightens his voice as he asks the car if they want to stop somewhere to get food. Cade is apparently excited about that, has all sorts of opinions.

"Nic?"

"I don't care." He hates when I say that, and before all of this, it's not something I would have said to him —at least not in that tone. It's disrespectful. But my dad isn't who I once believed him to be, and he doesn't deserve my respect.

"Let's go to Gino's!"

I scoff, once again looking at Cade like he's a literal piece of shit. Because he is. "That place is gross."

"You just said that you don't care where we go," he huffs.

I grit my teeth. I did just say that. "Doesn't mean I want food poisoning."

"You don't—I've never gotten food poisoning from there. Liam and I eat there all the time. Literally every time we come down here."

I roll my eyes. He's so far up his best friend's ass it's ridiculous. "Yeah, well, your boyfriend isn't here. So I say we eat somewhere else."

"He's not—" he clamps his mouth shut, face getting red. It makes me smile, which only makes his blush worse. "Not everyone is gay, Nicolas."

"That's true," I shrug, ignoring the dig at my sexuality and his use of my full name. "But you are. For Liam." I turn my head back towards the road before he can respond.

Honestly, I mean that. He likes his best friend a little too much. He talks about him obsessively and looks at him with total heart eyes. Defends him with his whole chest when I so much as mention the guy.

"Shut the *fuck* up," he shoves at me, the impact

blunt and jarring.

"What the hell? Keep your hands to yourself," I sneer, rubbing at my shoulder like I can actually remove that touch. Guess he inherited that trait from his mom.

"Boys!" my dad snaps, and Cade stills. "Nic, don't make me turn this car back around. I'll leave you at your—"

"Fine! Do it. That's what I want." But he knows that.

"It's what everyone wants," Cade adds, and I don't even feel the need to respond.

It *is* what everyone wants. I don't know why my dad insists on dragging me to his house, but all it does is shove his new family down my throat. Force them to put up with me. Forces me to watch them be the kind of family mine used to be.

It hurts. It's suffocating. I can feel my heart rate quickening, the familiar feel of ants crawling all over my face. I don't want to leave my mom behind like he did. Cold and alone and drowning because that's what she's doing right now.

"I don't want to go, *Anton*." My voice is shaky. I don't want that. I don't want these people to hear that. So I dig my fingers in my thigh, letting the sharp burn ground me. It clears my head almost instantly, a crutch I shouldn't be so relieved to have. "I *want* to stay home." I close my eyes and can't help but resume worrying about my mom, who's been alone for mere minutes.

It hasn't been long at all, but it's hard to deal with because *I* left her alone.

"If he wants to stay at his mom's, I don't see why—"

"Don't talk about her." My voice is low as I speak to just Cade, and I don't feel nearly as tough as I sound. But I keep my fingers pressed hard into my leg—a bead of sweat on my forehead and a coldness blanketing my skin emphasizing just how much it hurts. How much pain I'm in. I think about how much I wish I felt that pain like I used to as my breaths come faster, shallower.

Tracey turns the radio up, like that'll somehow stop my dad from ranting. But he's pissed, no longer willing to turn around. Because, of course, now that he knows that's what I actually want, he's against the idea.

"Nic," Cade whispers, but I ignore him. I stare ahead at the back of his mom's seat, trying hard to ignore all of them—him, his mom, my dad and his berating. "*Nic,*" his hand grips mine, and I jerk it out of his hold.

"*Stop.* Touching me." What even is that?

"You're bleeding." He's still whispering, and maybe that's why it takes me a second to understand him, but when I do, my eyes fall to my lap.

Oh. I should have bandaged it, but it's been a few days. There shouldn't be that much. A lot of times, they don't bleed at all. This is... it's a lot.

"Nic, maybe you should—"

"Maybe you should mind your own business." I expect him to look annoyed. Maybe mad.

But he just keeps staring at me in a way nobody has looked at me in a long time. Like he's worried. It makes me uncomfortable. I kind of want to hit him, but I don't want to draw any attention back here.

"It's fine," I rush to say, but he doesn't seem convinced. "Don't make this a thing."

He takes a beat, his thoughts loud as he considers the situation—so loud that they smother the sound of mine. I don't understand. Why does he even care?

His head nods after a bit, moving slowly and again, I'm confused. I'm relieved but also... something close to unsettled. Maybe disappointed.

Nobody ever worries about me.

He looks at my leg again, where I have a palm lying flat over the blood that's still seeping through the fabric, and this time, his head shakes.

"Nic is bleeding," he says loudly, voice steady as he looks away from me. "A lot—his leg."

I want to be pissed, but I'm just... tired. *I'm so tired.*

And when my dad turns his head to look at me, I take the easiest deep breath I've taken in a few years.

One

Cade

"**C**adence, please stop looking so sad. Your busted-up face and pout are making me... you're bumming me out. Stop it!"

"Baby, fuck off."

"I can't!" he whines, walking into my room and sitting crosslegged on Liam's bed—or what *was* Liam's bed.

It's not his bed anymore. He's just gone. Left because I fucked up and *kissed him* like an idiot, and now he hates me. Probably.

God, that was stupid. I'm kind of glad his boyfriend punched me. I deserve the busted face. So, *so* stupid.

"I can't leave you alone when you're being so pathetic."

I glare.

"Do you want to go to the movies with me?"

I roll my eyes, huffing a laugh. "Baby, it's not your job to make me less..." I don't finish. I'm not even sure how to finish. Less sad? Embarrassed? Fucking stupid?

"But... they're doing a special showing of The Outsiders."

"Oh, okay." I force a smile—my instincts trying to keep me from doing it even though my lip is fully healed now—as I sit up and toss my legs over the edge of my bed. "You want to go watch one of your shitty old movies and have no friends lame enough to go with you."

"Please?" He gives me his best version of puppy dog eyes. "It's not even a musical."

I'll never tell him that I actually enjoyed Little Shop of Horrors, and The Outsiders doesn't sound so bad right now. I happen to like that movie anyway. So, as long as it's not an attempt to cheer me up... "Yeah, okay."

"That's why you're my favorite roommate." He beams.

"Oh, does Liam leaving mean I've been promoted?"

"Your face looks a lot better," he says, a clear deflection, but whatever.

"Gee, thanks."

It still looks a little fucked, but yeah, it is getting better. The bruises under my eyes are fading, now an ugly greenish-yellow instead of dark purple. It's been a week since the *incident*, so there's pretty much no swelling, but it's not attractive. The stitch on the inside of my lip is gone, dissolved already, and it doesn't hurt to talk anymore.

It really was a case of it-looks-worse-than-it-is, but

still. People stare at me, and it's humiliating. Even with most people not knowing why I got my face pummeled.

"Have you... talked to Liam's boyfriend at all?"

I shake my head. "I've barely even talked to Liam."

"That's... he's kind of dumb. Literally everyone— except him and Logan—knew you had a... thing for him."

I tilt my head back, looking away from him because I just don't know what to say to that.

"But you didn't deserve a broken nose. Sebastian hasn't even apologized?"

"No. I—" I cringe. "I don't need an apology. I deserved it." Really, it feels like *I* need to apologize. Again. *Why the fuck did I do that?*

"Yeah, but he shouldn't have hit you."

"I kissed his boyfriend." My stomach flips, but I barrel through the immediate misery those words trigger. "Tell me you wouldn't try to fuck someone up if you caught them all over your boyfriend."

"My fists aren't really made for conflict, y'know?"

I appreciate him not echoing any mentions of the kiss. I keep waiting for other people to bring it up, but it's like we're all just avoiding the specifics. Or they are. Sometimes, it feels like I just can't help but bring it up.

I feel guilty. And it doesn't feel like anything was actually resolved, so the feeling just won't go away. I know why I did it. Years of pent-up what-ifs ran through my head all at once, and I just... kissed him.

I know that to everyone else, it seems like

something I did out of the blue, but it's been on my mind for years. Liam. My best friend. Something I always deemed off-limits until suddenly I saw a maybe. He likes guys now, and I just had to try. And he was pushing me away. It was hard to talk to him because he was hiding, dealing with his seemingly new sexuality, and neither of us knew how to navigate around that.

It felt like I was losing him. So, I had to try.

My timing was a little off, and I embarrassed the fuck out of myself, but at least I know. At least I'm not left hoping for something that's clearly never going to happen anymore.

But I might be losing him anyway.

God. I really wish I was still lying down.

"They're dainty." Baby holds his hands out like he's modeling jewelry. Maybe his hands aren't built for bashing faces in, but I can't imagine him— or anyone—just being okay with the situation I put Liam's bulky boyfriend in.

"You wouldn't try to bite them?"

"No, I told you. That's my love language." He gives me a toothy grin, flashing his weapon of choice at me as he pushes his hair off his forehead.

"Well, shit. You must really love me," I say, thinking of all the many, *many* times he's bitten me. Sure as fuck doesn't feel like love when he does it, though.

He rolls his blue eyes at me, choosing not to confirm or deny it. "Come on," he slaps the bare mattress before getting up. "Let's go watch Matt Dillon in his prime up on the big screen."

"You should drive my car."

"Why would I do that?"

"Because I don't want to drive," I tell him, finally getting out of bed. "But I also don't want to sit in your tiny ass Fiat."

He scoffs. "Rude. I don't want you in the pimp mobile anyway." He snags the keys I hold out for him, and all I have to do is shove my feet in a pair of sneakers so we can leave.

∞ ∞ ∞

"Hey, Mom."

"Hey, sweetie. Real quick, I wanted to talk about Christmas."

"Okay." I smile, knowing she's going to lay it on heavy, beg me to come stay for the break. I told her I wanted to skip on Thanksgiving and stay here because it was only a four-day weekend anyway, but she and Anton drove down here the day after. To make up for it. But when she asks if I want to spend Christmas with her, I can't even imagine not saying yes.

"Okay. Okay, great," she chimes and I can hear the smile in her voice through the phone. I swear I can hear it grow as she goes on and on about plans. She wants to go on a small vacation, but at the moment,

I don't really care. I just let her talk, barely giving any input until she changes the topic altogether. "How're you doing?"

I pause, trying to decide how much I should tell her. "Not that great."

My mom and I are close, but not the kind of close that requires us to talk every single day. She has her own life, and I have mine. So, I definitely have some shit to clue her in on.

She's known that I'm bi almost as long as I've known—cried with me when I begged her to keep my secret and tried to convince me that it wasn't a big deal. But she knew about my pathetic crush on Liam way before I did. She knew my reasons for keeping quiet. It's not... I haven't always wanted him like that. He used to just be someone I thought of as a brother, so for me to just one day decide I wanted more...

It had royally fucked with my head. Honestly, he's kind of clueless. I'd agonize over how obvious I was being at times but he never once seemed aware. How he didn't know is beyond me.

But my mom knew, so telling her all the sordid deets isn't a hardship right now. It might even feel kind of nice to get it off my chest—cathartic, in a way.

"I'm so sorry, Cade." She means it. I can hear it in her mom-voice and can't help but let it comfort me.

"It's okay. Really." I sigh, mostly believing it. I'm in this weird in-between where I feel relieved but also antsy. There's just too much up in the air. He's my best friend, and I hardly see him. Talk to him.

"It will be." She says it with so much sincerity that

it's hard not to believe her. Then she starts talking about moving on and finding someone else, a nice guy or gal, and I roll my eyes more than once throughout the whole thing. But it makes me feel better just to listen to her and know that she's listening to me too.

I do not tell her that Sebastian—the big, sexy, tatted motherfucker who has pretty much stolen my best friend—punched me in the face for kissing Liam. Like most sons, I've learned what sorts of things I need to keep from my mom. Saves us both a lot of unnecessary stress.

"He moved out?" This seems more surprising to her than the fact that Liam, the guy she's known as straight for almost fifteen years, is actually into dudes. "How long has he been dating this boy?"

Mothers, I roll my eyes—again. "It doesn't really matter," I tell her—because *we're talking about me here, Mom.* "He's gone, and now I either have to pay more in rent or find a roommate." And neither option has me all that pumped to be alive right now.

Liam tried to discreetly set it up with Baby to where he would still pay a share, but that's stupid. I don't want that.

She gasps, the sound dramatic enough that it makes me jump a little.

"What?"

"I have *the best* idea. It's perfect!" She starts babbling, her voice getting quieter as she starts talking to who I assume is my stepdad, Anton. Getting all giddy and shit about something I'm not clued in on just yet.

"Mom," I try to cut through her excitement. "Mom!"

"Oh, sorry. I was just telling Anton that—well, I have a roommate for you!"

"Wait, what?"

"Okay, so promise to hear me out first."

"Mother." What the hell?

"Nicolas needs—"

"No." I don't need to hear her out. The answer is no. I'd way rather pay more money and have to work more or even just go find some stranger to share a room with than let Nic move in. He'd be *here*. In my room. Not even ten feet away. "Mom, no," I say again, just so there's no confusion.

"Cade, don't be like that. He needs a place to stay. He wants to go back to school, and I don't see why—"

"Mom! He hates my guts." I'm not exactly his biggest fan, either. He doesn't just hate *me*. He cannot stand my mom, and I find it hard to tolerate someone who so blatantly disrespects the woman who single-handedly raised me until I was thirteen. I understood his disdain at first, but as the years went on and he just got nastier and nastier, I grew tired of his shit. I can't even believe she thought it was a good idea to ask this of me.

And I do not want to hear his sob story. She's always felt sorry for him, maybe guilty for having played a part in his parents' failed marriage, but I don't share the same sympathies. There's no point in having sympathy for someone who doesn't want it. Pretty sure me feeling sorry for him is part of why he hates me so much anyway.

"He doesn't hate you," she lies. "That was years ago." She doesn't even believe that. I can hear it in her voice, how much she knows that it's not true. If there's one thing Nicolas Aldana can do, it's hold a fucking grudge. "Come on. Anton was planning to help him pay his dorm fee, but it's cheaper if he just moves in with you. Please?"

Oh, *gross*. I hate when she says that word.

"We were thinking of renewing our vows and finally having a wedding, and I was so excited—you know how badly I've wanted a wedding! But just... well, with Nic here, I haven't been able to do any planning. It wouldn't be right."

I can hear the phantom begging, can feel it smothering me. She has woefully complained about their lack of a real wedding since they got married. So, she's correct in saying that I know how badly she wants one. And I feel for her—maybe—but fuck. Nic is hard to deal with. He's just a moody little shit who does nothing but listen to bad music and brood all over the place. But I don't want to hear another *please* from my mom.

And really, I do need a roommate. I don't pay for school, but I do pay rent, and honestly, not even that much. So, it's been nice being able to set most of the money I make working aside. I just want to be set for when I graduate. I have plans and shit.

"I guess," I concede, my head shaking. I can hardly even believe this is my life right now. Liam was supposed to be here. We had planned on being roommates years before we even applied to college. "I'll have to ask Baby, though."

But I know he's going to say yes, can feel that word dragging me deeper into this sour mood I've been stuck in lately. He was just asking what I wanted to do about the room and rent situation a few hours ago.

"He said yes!" She practically giggles as she talks to her husband about it. It's kind of hard to be happy for her when I feel so miserable.

I make sure to move the phone before I let out a heavy sigh. The last time I saw Nic, he was still very much pissed at me for being the reason he was moved out of his mom's house—which is bullshit. Things had to of been fucked up to begin with, and I had nothing to do with that. I don't know the full story and I don't want to know the full story, but basically, I'm the bane of his existence. And all because I had the audacity to give the tiniest fuck about his well-being.

So much for shit being okay.

I don't mean to be dramatic, but basically, my life sucks ass.

Two

Cade

"Y ou want to go on a diet?" This would be news to me. For as long as I can remember, Liam has hated dieting. He hates having to regulate his food intake, having to say no to foods he actually wants to eat, and choke down shit he'd never look at again if it were up to him. So, us being at the gym to talk to the dietician-slash-nutritionist is... well, it's a mystery.

"No," he says gruffly, glaring at the glass door that the dude we're supposed to be meeting can definitely see us through. "Bash thinks it's a good idea."

"*What the fuck?* Your boyfriend wants you to go on a diet, and no part of you thought—"

"No! Not at all. Bash is—he thinks I have an unhealthy relationship with food." His cheeks flame, something I've seen a lot over the years but definitely more often now that he can't help but talk about his precious *Bash* every chance he gets.

A forced grin tugs at my lips as he palms the

back of his neck, another nervous tick that I'm very familiar with. The things he's saying aren't exactly big shockers. He definitely does have issues related to food, but nothing I've ever seen has warranted him meeting with an *expert*. But I also didn't think I'd ever seen anything that hinted at him liking dick, so what do I know?

"He suggested I see this... person." He shrugs, clearly uncomfortable with the whole thing. "Bash is not an asshole. He's actually really sweet."

The little smile on his reddened face makes me want to roll my eyes, but I don't do that. But sure. I'm sure the guy who broke my nose is a real sweet guy.

"Okay. Well, are we going in?"

"I——no. No." He shakes his head, but I'm pretty sure that's the whole reason I'm even here. "Sorry. It's just me going in."

"Liam, then why did I even come?" I swear to god, if he couldn't come up with a better excuse to see me than this, I'll—

"I'm just nervous, okay?" He turns toward me and the look on his face has me shutting my mental mouth. "Can you just hang out? I won't be long."

I want to be shitty and ask him why his super sweet boyfriend couldn't come with him—especially since he's the one who set this thing up—but he does look nervous. And really, even if he is throwing me a bone, don't I want to take it? The alternative is just blowing him off, and that means shoving a bigger wedge between us.

And maybe there are things I don't know. Maybe he

really needs this.

"I'll just go for a jog, I guess." I nod towards the rest of the gym.

"Thank you." He says it so seriously that I kind of feel like an asshole for having an attitude about it. Liam pulls this feeling from me quite a bit, actually. Guilt.

He doesn't even do it on purpose. He's just so... gentle. He's this six-foot-one used-to-be baseball player who makes people want to protect him and shit. There are other reasons—more taxing and misery-inducing reasons—that I feel guilty even just looking at him sometimes, but I'm not going to let myself dwell on all of that right now.

"Sure. I'll be here when you're done." I almost want to ask if Sebastian is working—meaning is he here, and am I going to have to look at him or possibly inadvertently piss him off just by existing in his proximity—but I keep it in.

As soon as he walks through the glass door in front of us, I walk around the corner and beeline to the treadmills. I want to run—sprint and work off some of the itchiness plaguing my very being—but I'm not really dressed for that. And I don't feel like doing any warmups or stretches, so I just walk.

I can't stop myself from looking for Liam's boyfriend, and my eyes find him pretty much instantly. Sebastian is hard to miss—tall with a million tattoos. He looks like he's always mad at someone. He's in the room he's almost always in, doing his trainer thing and looking annoyingly hot while doing it.

I thought about going for it at one point, asking him out. Got brave enough to ask him what his name was and then walked away when he told me with a glare. But really, I chickened out because of Liam. I'm not really in the closet. Well, I'm definitely not now that Liam knows, but before this whole mess I was kind of somewhere in the middle. I went to clubs, usually Class, and had quick hookups with guys whose names I don't remember—rarely even learned —every so often, but when it came to my best friend, I made *sure* he didn't know.

I was careful. Sneaky even. I was scared, honestly. I really thought there was a big chance that he'd be disgusted with me if he knew. Liam has just always had that kinda-sorta homophobic feel about him. And even if he hadn't been grossed out by me, I thought it'd clue him in on all the more-than-platonic feelings I had for him, and I could not handle that. The only reason I'm doing it now is because I have no choice.

I wonder how different shit would have been if I'd actually gone for it with Sebastian. Or better yet, gone for it with Liam years ago.

I have to force myself to look away, tired of bumming myself out. I get into the groove of mindlessly walking, zoning out as I take comfort in the atmosphere of the gym I've been coming to for the past couple of years.

I don't know how much time has passed before my phone vibrates in my back pocket. It's a text from an unsaved number, but the message tells me pretty point-blank who it is.

where tf is apartment 13???

When I don't answer him in the point-two seconds he wants, I get another one. And then another.

And now he's calling.

"The odd numbers are all on the right side," I say immediately, making sure to speak before he can start his bitching. "Number thirteen is in the second set of apartments, on the bottom floor. The thirteen is pink and pretty big, so—Nic?"

He hung up on me.

"*Dick*," I mutter to myself. I've been pretty lucky not having to directly communicate with him—my mom or his dad usually being the ones I talk to, but I guess all that's over now. Because he's here. I really fucking hope he's not an asshole to Baby or Logan.

I shoot a text to Baby to warn him that our newest roommate is there and then fight the urge to apologize. I haven't really explained the Nic lore to him. Maybe he's not a massive prick these days. I mean, I doubt it, but it's possible.

I haven't seen him in years. When I go visit on holidays or whatever, he's just been... gone. Somewhere else. My mom will give me updates here and there, but mostly, Nic is hardly even an afterthought. He's just someone I vaguely know, someone who thinks I ruined his life.

I had no clue why Nic's leg was bleeding. I had a feeling it was something bad when he reacted the way he did, but how was I supposed to know that telling on him would lead to him being forcibly removed from his mom's? *Nobody* saw that coming.

I still don't know the full story. If anyone had bothered actually looking at him—seeing him and the muted look on his face, the sweat on his hairline, chapped lips, and dark eyes—they'd have known something was wrong. I only know that Nic was hurting himself, and Carrie, his mom, was *not fully present*. Asking either my mom or Anton for details felt too taboo, especially with the way they tiptoed around the topic. And asking Nic, the guy whose hate for me went from one hundred to one thousand after that whole thing, was not an option.

And he dipped two years after that. Up and left the place he refused to ever call home. The only info I ever heard about him came from our parents.

I don't hate him, despite what he thinks. I don't even really know enough about him to hate him. I just have enough shit going on, and I really don't want him and his drama piling onto the mess.

Liam comes out after what feels like a small forever but is actually twenty-something minutes and tells me he wants to talk to his boyfriend before we go. I can't tell if he's just trying to act like I didn't put my lips on his ten days ago or if he truly doesn't care, but either way, it's driving me crazy. It feels too weird to witness whatever goes on between those two so I make my way out of the gym and wait for him by my car.

"You ready?" I ask about five minutes later as he walks around up to the passenger side to get in it.

"Yeah. Let's stop for some food."

"Okay," I agree, not bothering to ask him where to go as I climb in and start the car. He's one of those people who like to drive me insane by having zero clue where they want to eat, even if they're the ones who suggested we do so. If he knew what he wanted, he'd have just named the place. "How was the meeting?"

"It was okay. He used to be a food therapist—which apparently is a legit thing. We really just talked about my eating habits and how they make me feel, so nothing crazy."

Thinking about this a little more in-depth, it's not all that surprising. I found a stash of junk food in his closet when we were teens once, and when I mentioned it, his face had gone pale. I just never brought it up again. Maybe I should have, but from where I stood, he was a healthy jock who just didn't get to eat sweets very often.

"Maybe you should see a professional? Someone who is *currently* a food therapist."

"Nah," he shakes his head, clearly feeling certain about this. "I'm not... I just have all this freedom now, y'know? I just have to get used to it not needing to be a secret when I eat a fucking piece of cake or something. And this guy is cool. And cheap, so I can meet with him a few more times. He works on diet plans with people trying to lose weight and gain weight, but he also just listens. He said as long as I'm honest with him, he'll do his best to recognize habits, and if he spots any unhealthy ones, he'll advise me on... I don't know exactly. It won't get that far."

The way he talks about it makes it seem like it's

maybe a bigger deal than he's willing to admit. I open my mouth to ask if he's sure he's got this, but he speaks first.

"What do you have going on for the rest of the day?"

I cock my head at him, unsure how I want to answer. I can feel him asking to hang out, but I'm not all that certain I want to—that I can even deal with that right now. Maybe it's messed up to not want to be around him immediately after he sort of admitted to having an eating disorder, but things *are* messed up between us right now.

"Not much, but I should probably get home. Nic just got here, and I don't want him to—"

"Nic—like, your stepbrother? That Nic?"

"Oh. I never told you." I let out a rueful laugh as I run a heavy hand down my face. I haven't had the chance to tell him more like. I've only known about this for three days, and we haven't talked that much since he moved out. "He's your replacement."

"What do you mean?"

"He's moving in." When all he does is gape at me, I shrug. "My mom asked."

"And you said yes?"

"She asked nicely." I breathe another short laugh out through my nose with a shrug at the look on his face. Nic and Liam don't really get along either—or they didn't. I don't think Nic gets along with anyone.

"I'm... sorry."

"It's not your fault, Liam. And it's not that big of a deal." It really isn't. Between work and school, I don't even spend that much time in my room. It's been years since I've lived with Nic, but from what I can remember, he spends most of his time brooding in bed, listening to shitty music. As long as I stay out of his way he pretty much ignores me.

It'll probably be harder to do now that we share a bedroom. I only have the past to go by, but I need to get it in my head that we're not sixteen years old anymore. I knew Nic *then*—and only kind of. I definitely don't know who he is today.

"Well, still. You're going to be living with an asshole. That sucks."

"You would know," I say, nodding my head and smiling as I let myself tease him about this.

He rolls his eyes, blushing a little which in turn triggers a roll of mine. He's so smitten. It almost gives me secondhand embarrassment. Dude is a total simp for a guy who has the emotional range of a rock.

It also—a tiny bit—hurts my feelings. I've been around for years. Most of our lives. Why wasn't *I* his bi-awakening? What's so wrong with me?

But I'm ignoring those thoughts. Trying to anyway.

∞∞∞

"**W**here is he?"

"You mean your fine as fuck stepbrother? Cade." Baby leans forward, palms on his knees. "You should have warned me."

"What do you—gross. Baby, no," I scold. "He's... bad."

"He's something alright." He laughs as he leans back in his spot on the couch. His face sobers quickly, all traces of humor gone as he deadpans, "I can fix him."

I can't tell if he's serious. Either way, I'm annoyed. What the fuck is it with assholes getting all the attention? Liam and Sebastian, and apparently Baby and Nic. Especially when Baby thinks it's funny to constantly make jokes about me being the ugliest dude in the apartment. "That's not a thing. This—you and *Nic*—that's not happening."

"Well, yeah, that's probably true. I don't actually have a bad boy kink. I usually avoid them." He shrugs. "But Nicolas doesn't seem *that* bad. Kind of shy, maybe. Moody. But, I mean, he's out of my league anyway."

"What? That is not true. You're—"

"Stop. I'm a solid ten outta ten, I know this. But that dude in your bedroom is—" He fans his face, being all kinds of annoying about it. "How into dudes are you exactly? Because no marriage would have kept *me* from—"

"I'm done talking to you." I walk away, shaking my head at the fuckery that was.

"I'm just sayin'. Stepbrother porn is popular for a reason!"

I roll my eyes just as I reach my door, not thinking things through as I open it. My body lags as I remember Nic is supposed to be in here, but he's not. Both beds are empty, though what used to be Liam's is no longer bare.

I twitch when the bathroom door opens.

"Nic?" I don't know why I bother asking, but fuck. "You got..." *Bigger* is what I almost say, but I manage not to embarrass myself. He was eighteen the last time I saw him and both shorter and skinnier than me. A gauntly looking emo kid with patchy skin and hair.

But, *fuck*. Not anymore. He looks just as tall as me and definitely packing the kind of muscle mass I wouldn't have ever assumed was capable for him.

"Get out."

"*What?* It's my room."

He has a gift. Never has a single person pissed me off so instantaneously like that. And with so little effort, too.

"It's also mine now, and I need to get dressed. So, fuck off."

I almost flinch. I—yeah. He's naked. He's naked and wet and has nothing but a big towel wrapped around his waist to keep shit from getting hella awkward.

Well, no. That's not true. It kind of does feel

awkward. I haven't seen him in years, but I've *never* just had a front-row seat to the guy's nipples like this. His skin-thing is more prominent than I'd have guessed now that I can see his chest. He even has one spot, under his collar bone on his pec, that looks like a small jagged heart. Probably a good representation of what his actual heart looks like. I should maybe look away, but also... "No. It's my room. You can get dressed in the bathroom."

He scoffs as he steps in front of me. "Just get out, Cade."

I stare for a moment, the utter audacity of this guy leaving me at a loss for words. I don't remember his eyebrow being split like that, about a third of it white, like his hair.

"Stop fucking drooling and get out."

This time, I scoff, my face heating at the accusation he's throwing out there with his deep voice. I don't know how to respond to that. I open my mouth to speak, make myself deny it or something, but he's suddenly shoving me, and the door is shut in my face not even a full second later.

I try to open it back up, but my hand isn't quick enough. He flips the lock, and I'm left to stand there with my mouth agape. Stunned.

What the fuck?

There's just too much about this situation that's irritating the absolute hell out of me. Nic is somehow exactly nothing and everything I expected. An asshole? Definitely. A scrawny-looking kid with his white-streaked hair overgrown and covering his eyes?

Not exactly. Not anymore.

I get what Baby was going on about just minutes prior. I get it. I can't deny how good he looks, and who the fuck saw that coming? Not me. He's just all grown up and shit, and it's confusing me. The fucker might actually be a little bigger than me. I'm not even a small guy, but he only needed one hand, one solid shove to move me out of the room.

And it's my fucking room!

Three

Nic

I ignore Cade when he starts knocking on the door, fists heavy as he pounds away. I only just manage not to let him annoy me. He hasn't changed one bit. Cocky and muscled with that ever-present himbo look on his stupid fucking face.

Okay. So clearly, I fail at not letting him get to me. But it can't be helped. He's always pressed *all* the wrong buttons, every single one I've got. And there's a lot of them. His very presence pisses me off pretty much the split second I see him, and that has not at all changed. There's just something too easy about him. The very air that surrounds Cadence Howard is *light*. Like he has no worries, nothing to stress over. Like he's not forced to carry the kind of weight I am.

And he isn't. He breathes easier than I do because he can. Because his air isn't something dense and suffocating. He'll never understand just how much he's lucked out. I lost a parent when he gained one.

He hasn't changed. At least not in appearances.

His dark brown, wavy hair is a medium-length mess on his head, just like always. Same muddy green eyes with lashes much longer than necessary surrounding them. The only real noticeable difference is that the divot in his chin is more noticeable than it once was now that he's lost the bit of baby fat he had.

His good looks were one of the things that made me hate him when I moved into their house five years ago. He's nothing like me, and all of the differences were so glaring and *better* that I just had to resent him. He was a good son and I was a disappointment, and we certainly looked the part.

Even people at school flocked around him. Why wouldn't they? He was nothing but smiles—as long as he wasn't looking at me—and I was the opposite. *Disturbed*. My dad actually said that once. It made people—my dad and his new wife, namely—not want to be around me. Even if they were the ones who insisted I be there. Cade was easy for my dad to deal with, to *love*, and I just… made shit hard.

It got easier once I accepted things as they were. My mom was alone, and I was alone, and I just couldn't do anything about it. So I put up with it—learned to not feel.

When Tracey suggested this arrangement, my immediate reaction was something so filled with dread that I was thrown off. It had been jarring to have any one feeling be so tangible, something I felt with my whole body. So, I lied. I told myself that I don't hate Cade, that I could handle living with him if it meant getting my shit together and learning how to feel again. Seeing him in person proves how big of a lie that was, but I have the chance to move forward. Move out of the limbo I've been bound to for a big chunk of my life, and I want that. I've sacrificed a lot for my mom. I see that now, and I want... more.

Or I think I do. Otherwise, why would I start therapy? Reach out to my dad? Some part of me doesn't want things to stay the same.

There are other parts of me that are missing, a hollowness that makes it hard to feel. And while it is hard, sometimes unbearably so, it's also not impossible. I do feel some things—sad, ugly things usually. But if I could somehow get to a point where the things I feel aren't always sad or ugly... well, why wouldn't I want that?

So, I'm here. In Cade's room. *Feeling* annoyed because he just happens to be real fucking good at inducing that particular emotion. Being here is temporary. I just need to get a job and save up so I can get my own place. As long as I stay in school—actually finish this time around—my dad said he'd help out. It's why I came so early and didn't wait until after the holidays. I wanted to get a good footing before I actually start school. By the time I do, I want to be on my own.

Well, not entirely. I know I have to make an effort not to be so... lonely. I have my Dad—or I'm trying to. Sometimes, I slip in my head and still refer to him as Anton, but I'm trying. And he is, too. He seems happy to do it even. He insisted on helping me out. With him giving me cash, I'm fairly certain that I can pull this off—be on my own. I mean, living with my mom was basically the same thing anyway. This won't be all that different, but it will hopefully be healthier.

I move quickly as I get dressed, pulling a pair of sweats on and being careful to spread the hemline enough to keep it from dragging over the tops of my thighs.

It's been years since those wounds were fresh, but the scars left over have made the skin there both oversensitive and unfeeling at once. It's uncomfortable. There's a lot of nerve damage surrounding them, and when anything touches those areas, it makes it hard not to cringe. One of my doctors said that there wasn't much I could do to avoid it. Hurting myself has left a lot of nerve endings all jumbled up, jagged. She said that when they're stimulated, my body is just stuck trying to make sense of the mess. Sometimes it hurts, but most of the time, it just feels so fucking strange. It makes my whole body want to recoil.

Cade can be as pissed as he wants to be. No way was I going to let him stay in here and gawk at the mess I've made of myself. And he would have. He couldn't take his eyes off of me, off my chest.

I've had vitiligo in some form my whole life, but— my hair and the spot on my forehead not included— it hadn't been as noticeable when he'd last seen me as it is now. Stress and age have made it worse. When my doctor told me those were likely the cause of its progression, it kind of cemented the idea that I don't have control of my life. And it's hard to expel those beliefs with the proof being right there every time I look at myself. But I'm trying to change that.

The topical corticosteroid she prescribed didn't really do anything except make my skin thin and give me acne, so I stopped using it. Looking at my arms has me wondering if maybe I should just try again. There's a mirror hanging on the door, and one look at it has me reaching back in my suitcase and digging around for a sweatshirt.

It's only once it's on that I finally unlock the door.

He tries to barrel past me, but I'm not as small as I was the last time he saw me, and pushing him out of the way is pretty easy.

"What's your problem?" His face is flushed as he straightens back up. He hit his back on the edge of the doorway, which I'm sure hurt more than he's willing to show. "You literally just got here and already—"

"I don't have a problem, little brother." I fight a smile when he glares at me, his mouth clamped shut as he takes that in. He's always hated when I call him that.

I've never said it with anything less than disgust in my voice and I get why he hates it. But it's my dad's fault that I say it at all. We were both thirteen when we met, but Cade's birthday being three weeks after mine prompted him to introduce Cade as my *new little brother*.

That in itself had felt like a slap in my mom's face, so I didn't really appreciate it either. She had just suffered a miscarriage that year, something that hit her hard—she lost a baby boy pretty late in the pregnancy. She'd rub her round belly and smile, telling me my little brother was in there. But he didn't make it.

At that age, I didn't fully understand the weight of a loss like that, but I'd seen the damage. It's how I mark the beginning of my mom's mental downfall, the avalanche that buried who she used to be. I thought it hit both of my parents hard, but Anton moved on pretty quickly.

But something about the way Cade had blushed when my dad had said *little brother* had fascinated me. And sometimes, if I said it just right, I could make my dad squirm too.

"*Don't* call me that."

This time, I can't keep the grin off my face. He's always been easy to rile up. It's another thing about him that hasn't changed.

When I don't offer the reaction he wants, he changes tactics. "Why are you even here, Nic? Your mom got sick of you and your shitty attitude? Can't say I blame her." He scoffs.

I guess some things have changed. Talking about my mom, bringing her up at all, was something he was too scared to do back then. The whole house had been, really.

"*Careful.*"

"I'm just saying. Pretty bad when not even your own mother wants to be around you. Now—"

I don't think about it as my hand closes around his throat, squeezing just hard enough to shut him up as I shove him against the door. "Watch yourself." It's only a second, maybe two before I push at his neck to get him away from me, but I get a satisfying view of his panic-stricken face all the same.

His head thuds against the wood as he chokes on a garbled noise. His widened eyes don't settle, like maybe he's shocked that I even did that in the first place. If I bothered to consider it, maybe I would be too. He was the one who had a problem with keeping his hands to himself back then. I was too small to really do anything about it, but we're evenly matched now.

And he pretty much asked for it. The topic of my mom being in this guy's mouth doesn't sit right with me. He's the reason I was taken away from her. I'd be doing her and myself a disservice by letting him run it now.

"I don't have a problem, and I don't want any, Cade." My voice is a lot calmer than I feel. Cade gives away too much with the way he reacts to things. I don't want to be the same, don't want to let him see things he just doesn't need to fucking see. "Leave me alone, and it'll stay that way."

He clears his throat, slowly straightening his spine once again, clearly feeling out of place in his own room. His hand moves, like maybe he wants to feel the skin my hand was just on, but it settles quickly at his side instead.

It's true. I'm not here for the drama, but if he wants my hand around his neck again, I guess I could find a way to be okay with that.

∞ ∞ ∞

"**A**lright, man. You're hired." Alex, the manager, smiles at me as he starts shuffling the papers he brought to the table.

"Just like that?" I had applied online as soon as Tracey told me about Cade's lack of a roommate, but I still expected more than just showing up and immediately getting the job.

He shrugs. "Sure. We called your references already, and everyone loves you. You've got experience, and we need the help."

"Well, shit." That was way easier than I thought it was going to be. "Oh, sorry," I say when he cocks a little admonishing brow at me, but the small smile on his lips tells me he's not actually mad. Still. This *is* an interview.

My fingers tap over my scars—a grounding technique that is mostly safe—doesn't hurt unless I make it. The thick fabric of my jeans doesn't let me feel the ragged ridges, but it's soothing, the slight pain muddied up by a phantom-like numbness. It can get to the point of overwhelming, too painful in certain spots at times, but right now it's good. Working at a diner, being on my feet all day, will make those sensations worse, but I have pain pills and lidocaine for that if it gets too bad.

"As long as you don't curse in front of the diners, you're good." He goes on to give me the rundown on the place, having me follow him to the office so he can get copies of my driver's license and social security card.

"Well, I have open availability until the spring semester starts. As soon as I have my class schedule, I can get that to you." I say it with as much aloofness as I can muster, but really, I'm hoping he isn't annoyed that I didn't tell him this before he told me I was hired.

I've put off school long enough. I only ever managed to do two semesters, so I'm way behind where I should be at twenty-one. I was stupid in thinking I could pull it off living with my mom.

I'd spent two years being forced away from her, rarely hearing from her and hardly ever seeing her. When I did talk to her, all of her updates involved her talking about getting help. Doing better. Even Paulina had said she was okay when I asked.

She lied. They both did. Turning eighteen meant freedom. It meant doing what I wanted, and she told me that she was okay. I visited, and the house was clean. She looked fed and happy. I had no reason not to believe her. So, I went to school. I left her—*again*—and when I came back, she was worse than when I'd been dragged away from her at sixteen.

My stomach pinches as I think about it. Those memories fucking suck. They aren't all like that. She really was a happy woman and a good mom for most of my childhood. But somehow, thinking about those memories is just as bad.

"Alright." He claps his hands together after handing me my things back. "So, you can start on Friday. I'll schedule you mornings for a while. That way, you can train with Cade."

"Cade?" The bitter laugh that leaves my lips can't be helped. *What are the fucking chances?*

"Yeah, he's one of our servers. He's the best."

The smile on this guy's face has my own fading. *The best.* "I'm sure he is."

Four

Cade

"What the hell is he doing?" I pull into the spot I always park in, only to have Nic pull in next to me. He's been following me the whole way here, and for some reason, I really doubt he got a sudden craving for Gerty's Grubhouse at six in the morning. Most likely, he followed me just to fuck with me.

Things have calmed way down in the two days he's been here. It's a little embarrassing, but him fucking choking me definitely did what he wanted— I got the message. I'm not proud of how much I let him get to me when he moved in all those years ago, but me hitting or shoving him just to shut him up— the few times he actually opened his mouth to speak anyway—wasn't out of the ordinary. So *Nic* doing *that* to me... well, I was surprised.

Surprised and maybe a little something else. I have no idea what it was I was feeling when his hand was wrapped around my throat. There were too many things all at once, making it impossible to pinpoint one thing. I mean, he *choked* me. Who does that? Besides, like psychos and serial killers. I look over at him when I hear his car door shut and decide that, yeah, that tracks. *Fucking psycho.*

He gets out and stands there for a moment. Just stands there like a weirdo, staring ahead at the front of the building. I don't expect it when he finally looks at me. I freeze, my mind and body buffering. It's not until he cocks a judgy as fuck brow at me that I react, face heating as I force my eyes away from him.

He is annoyingly hot, and I hate it. I *hate* it. My hookups with guys have been quick, nothing more than swapping blowjobs or handjobs in the backroom at Class or some other overcrowded club. So, being picky wasn't necessary, and outside of Liam, I'm not sure what my type is.

Nic looks nothing at all like my best friend. Liam is Hollywood pretty. Built and the kind of sweet that adds to his presence in a way that makes it a part of his appearance. Nic is the worst kind of fuckhead. He has issues, and I'm sure they're valid, but he makes it everyone else's problem. It adds an air of *ugly* to him that is too hard to ignore. Or it used to be.

Now he looks all hot and pisses me off and chokes me, and I'm just confused. Stepping out of my car has my belly dipping, angry anticipation bubbling all throughout my bloodstream as I get ready to face him.

"What are you doing here?" I sound fairly normal, so props for that.

"Working."

"That's——" That's the most unfunny joke I've ever heard. It's so unfunny that part of me knows he's serious. He even has a nametag on his black button-up.

"Alex says that you're training me."

"*Me?*"

"*You,*" he mocks.

I make myself take a deep breath and stop the comeback that wants to fall out of my mouth all willy-nilly. He's usually calm. Even when he puts his hand around my neck, he manages to do it with an icy demeanor. It makes me look stupid when I'm the only one sputtering and red-faced.

So, I swallow every word I want to say and stalk inside with him on my heels.

∞∞∞

"The new guy doing okay?"

I look at our hostess and frown.

"That bad, huh?" She laughs.

Actually, no. He's doing more than okay. And for whatever reason, that's the part that's irritating me. He does whatever I say, doesn't ask too many questions, and it's clear that he studied the menu. Plus, the clueless guests all love him. I'm pretty sure he's made more in tips than me. *Fucking morons.* They can't tell that an actual psychopath is taking their orders—don't see through his artificial smiles.

And honestly, I might be having a hard time seeing through them too. I don't know if I've ever seen him smile when it wasn't just something smug because he was irritating me to near death. So, these? These big, toothy grins and easy laughs?

I have to remember that he's the enemy. He once called my mom a whore to her face, and somehow it was me who got in trouble when I punched his arm. He called Liam and me homos every time Liam came to the house, and it stressed me out so much I just stopped letting him come over. Trying to fight over our shared bathroom as teens made mornings unbearable.

I realize that holding onto stuff he did as a teenager is a stupid reason not to like him, but there's also the part where he's just a horrible person. Rude and mean. Too bad his insides didn't have the same glow-up the rest of him did.

As a teen, he'd get mad that his dad and my mom were so nice to me all the time, but really, they coddled him. Let him get away with almost everything just because they were afraid to break his already fragile mind. And all the while, he acted like he was some mistreated prisoner—one with a really shitty attitude.

Glow-up aside, it's hard to get over the disdain I have for him.

But I'm not explaining all of this to Vivian.

"He's fine."

"He is that," she agrees, a coy little gleam on her

face that just should not be there this early in the morning.

Ew. "He's gay," I grunt and then ignore it when she pouts.

She starts talking about how cool and beautiful his skin is—a weird thing to say out loud, in my opinion—and I decide that I'm over it. He's not all that. It looks okay. It's kind of cool, yeah, but it's not cool enough to actually say so.

And beautiful?

My eyes trail him as he makes his way up the kitchen window, taking him in. I've always—rather begrudgingly—liked his hair. It's pitch black, except where those solid white streaks are, and I think most people would agree that it's nice—it's *definitely* not just me. He mostly has his dad's skin tone, a tawny shade of warm brown, but there are random patches of skin that are paler than even Baby's is. Light and creamy. All of him looks so soft, which is weird considering how rough his personality is. But he looks...

I huff, rubbing tiredly at my face just as a small group of senior citizens walk in. I'm supposed to be working, not fixating on Nic.

It's not crazy busy, not yet, and after I realized that Nic could handle his shit, I gave him his own section instead of letting him work off of mine. I was hoping to ignore him.

And that's what I do. Only it's a lot harder than it should be, his quiet presence demanding attention when he's not even doing anything except his job, and it is so fucking infuriating. There's no reason to be so irritated, but Jesus fuck. He's just the worst.

We're not even halfway through the shift when I see him pick a fifty-dollar bill off one of his tables. "Is that a tip?"

"Yup."

He gives me a cocky smirk, and that's how it starts. How *he* starts it, the fucker. We spend our last few hours trying to one-up each other—racing to put our orders in before one another, greeting customers as they walk in, and just all around giving these oldtimers the service of their goddamn lives.

When I see an order of country-fried steak pop up, I know it's not mine. He put his order in first, and sitting right next to it is a stack of pancakes that definitely doesn't belong to any of my tables. Does that stop me from grabbing the steak? Absolutely not. I'm on a mission as I walk toward my table and end up clipping his shoulder as we pass each other.

"Watch it," he complains.

But I'm already setting the stolen breakfast plate in front of my guest, smiling as the man thanks me. I feel a little giddy as I walk back and hear him asking the cook where it is. The plan is to feign innocence as I crowd his space, but the look he gives me—brows pitched low and a few strands of solid white hair falling over his frosty grey eyes—triggers a jolt of raw joy in me and suddenly, I'm all for simply owning it. I can feel the excitement his anger instills as it flares in the middle of my chest, and I am so ready for this.

"Oh, I took that." I shrug, and when he scoffs, I go

as far as beaming at him. "Whoops."

His full lips tilt at the corner, a tight half-smile paired with a humorless laugh that has my breath hitching. I don't even know why. That's all he gives me—a mirthless laugh and a sexy little pissed-off curve of his lips—and I swear it's the highlight of my day so far. Making him mad.

In the end, he wins. He counts his tips, but before he's even done, I can see that he's won. It's that fucking pretty privilege Liam is always talking about. Telling myself that it doesn't matter isn't all that effective. But still, it's a complete accident when I walk into him on the way to the crew room. It's happened a few times today, and in a restaurant setting, it's not uncommon. It's not a surprise when he gets mad, though. Tensions have been a little high—his fault, really but I haven't exactly helped the situation either.

"Watch it," I mimic his words from earlier.

"You're so fucking immature." He huffs, grabbing his keys and wallet out of the little cubby he dumped them in earlier.

I *am* immature. I can admit that, but I don't really see a problem with it. So, as I pass him again, it's not an accident when my shoulder hits his.

I expect the anger. I do not, however, expect it when he shoves me. My hands only just barely keep me from faceplanting into the cubbies.

"What the *fuck*, Nic?" I only just manage to turn around when the back of my head thuds against something hard, a warm hand keeping me there as I let out a hiss.

"Keep testing me, little brother."

"*Don't* call—"

His hand tightens, forcing me to move onto my tip toes. All my attention zeroes in on him, nothing but Nic plaguing my every sense. The tips of his fingers dig into a thick vein on the side of my neck, and I gasp, inhaling and somehow tasting him as I do. I can smell him—woody and laden with a spice that has my heartbeat thrumming. My nostrils flare, an attempt to find some more of that scent that ends up being nothing but a wasted breath.

I want him off of me. I open my mouth to try to speak, but he only presses harder over my Adam's apple, and then it's just a struggle not to gag as my hands clasp around his wrist. There's a pressure building in my temples—subtle, but it's there. Actual panic starts to take a physical form in my body, forcing a feeble little whine from between my parted lips that would embarrass me if I could only fucking think.

He's for sure overreacting. Nothing I've done today has warranted this. He's mental. Actually insane. He's telling me to leave him alone, but I haven't taken a breath in what feels like too long, so I can't listen. I try to move, but it only has him pressing into me, his body blanketing mine in an attempt to keep me still.

It's better, I realize. There's a swift, icy calm that tries to trick my nervous system into relaxing as his solid frame meets mine. It's real close to peaceful and so warm I close my eyes just to *feel* it.

And then it's gone. I'm left gasping for breath and coughing, gagging on oxygen as I try to blink through tears. He *choked* me. Blood rushes to my head so quickly I can hear it.

"You're—" Another cough cuts me off, and when my eyes come into focus, I give up. *Gone.* He left. Literally cut off my oxygen and dipped. He's certifiable. It feels a little like attempted murder. What a prick.

And for what? Because I bumped into his shoulder? Fucking nut.

I breathe deeply through the comedown and let my body regain awareness as I stand hunched over with my hands on my thighs. When I finally straighten up, I freeze.

I'm hard. My dick is fucking hard, pressed against my zipper in a way that hurts when I move.

"Hey, Cade."

My coworker's voice has me moving out of the room—unexpected and unwanted boner aside.

"How's it—"

"I gotta go." I hurry to leave, avoid looking at anyone as I walk through the restaurant, and hope like hell nobody looks at my dumb dick while it's being all sorts of dumb and refusing to relax.

I must have lost brain cells. I don't know how else to describe this.

I hesitate with my hand on my car door, grateful that my stepbrother's car is no longer here. I can't see my face all that clearly in the reflection on the window, but I can see enough to know that I'm glad he's not here to witness it. Face flushed and eyes glossy. I don't look at my neck. I don't even want to think about how I must have looked while he was giving me the marks that have to be there.

After long moments of nothing, I take a deep, well-earned breath as the pressure behind my zipper eases. Maybe it was adrenaline. A pissed-off fear boner. I was actually suffocating—*being* suffocated. That's gotta have all kinds of crazy, one-hundred percent unwanted effects on a body.

And it's definitely not boner-inducing. Not the good kind of boners, anyway.

God. Nic sucks. I haven't been this confused since Liam embraced the five-inch inseam fad. But, hell, at least Liam is *nice*. I may not know what my type is when it comes to guys, but *nice* is usually a factor no matter the gender. Nice people do not choke others.

He needs to cut it out. He better stop putting his hand on my throat like that, or I'll... shit, I don't even know.

Come. I'll probably come.

Five

Nic

He's probably embarrassed. That's got to be why he's still not home. I'm not sure why it bothers me so much, but I do wish we could just get this over with. Cade being gone is as much a relief as it is absolutely maddening. He makes me crazy when he's not even here. I keep waiting, expecting him to walk his bratty ass through the door at any second and tell me he's going to tell my dad on me or something.

I shouldn't have done it, but fuck. He asked for it. I tried to ignore him, but he did not make it easy. He made it impossible, actually.

I groan through clenched teeth, not wanting to voice any of my frustrations. I called him immature, but I wasn't exactly the picture of sophistication either.

But he *did* ask for it. Practically begged me to react—made sure I did by going on and on and on. Bumping into me, stealing tables, stealing food. I may be immature, but he's a toddler.

I might have overreacted, though. A little bit.

I don't know how to feel about what I did when the dam finally broke. The little warning squeeze I gave him two days ago was nothing compared to what I did a few hours ago. *That* was assault. Violent.

I just wanted to shut him up and teach him a lesson. I didn't expect it to backfire like that. Punch me? Sure. That makes all the sense there is. Pop a fucking woody against my thigh?

Yeah, I still don't really understand the logistics of that.

I used to tease him whenever I could about his obsession with Liam, and I definitely had my suspicions. But I never had any concrete proof to confirm. As far as I know, Cade is straight.

The music playing in my ears is quiet enough that I hear it when my new roommates start laughing out in the hall, the closed door keeping me out of the loop. When I recognize one of the muffled voices as Cade's, I'm moving.

I don't like confrontation, but I like avoiding confrontation even less. All that does is cause stress, and I'd really rather just rip the bandaid off.

I can hear him speaking to Baby before I pull the door open.

"What is this?" Baby places a hand on the side of Cade's neck—or tries to—making Cade flinch. The move has me feeling a conflicting mix of smugness and guilt. "Are those hickeys? What the heck was goin' on over at Gerty's?" Baby is overjoyed at the notion that someone was sucking on Cade's skin, but I'm pretty sure it's just from my fingers digging into his soft flesh. I can't see the marks, but I know they're there.

I'm not crazy—I didn't really want to suffocate him. Not at first. I just wanted to prove a point, maybe scare him. I was holding him with a purpose, being deliberate in trying not to actually suffocate him. Him staying cocky had my hand acting on its own, squeezing where a normal person would have let go.

To be fair, I don't think a normal person would have done any of that to begin with.

Cade denies Baby's accusation but offers no explanation, and it's obvious he's grateful Baby is nice enough not to press the issue. Instead, he turns to me, something Cade is actively avoiding.

"And where were you, Nicolas? I needed someone tall earlier, and somehow, all of my tall roommates were gone."

"Working. Got a job at Gerty's Grubhouse." I love the way this little twink's eyes light up when I say it, the way he snaps his attention back to Cade and zeroes in on his neck. It played out exactly how I wanted.

"Oh. I see."

"You don't—you see *nothing*," Cade bites, placing a palm on his bruises before quickly dropping his hand, realizing that all he's doing is drawing more attention to what he wants to hide.

"Okay. Sensitive." Baby side-eyes me, a playful little smile on his face. "But then, I guess that many hickeys would be, huh?"

He thinks I kissed my stepbrother. That's—hm. It bothers me, but compared to the truth, I guess it's okay. He most likely wouldn't understand. I'm not even sure that I do.

"Do you want to go to Class with us tonight?" Baby effectively changes the subject.

"Class?"

"It's a gay club."

That has my eyes moving to Cade again because why would he be going to a gay club? "You're going?" I ask, wanting some clarification.

The composure he was wearing cracks when he looks at me, his lips pursing as he fights his anger. Or maybe it's not anger but embarrassment? Both?

"Yes," he grinds out, triggering an involuntary tick in my jaw. It seems he learned no lesson.

I decide that I don't care if he's developed a liking for dick over the years and focus my attention back on Baby. "Yeah, I'll go."

I actually didn't know that's what I was going to say, but it's a done deal. I'm going. Fuck knows why, but maybe it'll be fun.

Of course, Cade is standing a foot away to remind me why that's a crazy thought to have.

He scoffs, moving into the room awkwardly in an attempt not to touch me as he goes. But I'm taking up the doorway, which means he is once again knocking into me. He has no fucking manners, but then I remember who his mom is, and I suppose that makes sense.

The only reason he gets to shut the door with me

still in the hallway is because Baby does this thing where he just doesn't shut up, and I get stuck listening to him babble about what kind of club he's dragging me to tonight.

I barely listen. Cade is going to a gay club, and I can't get over it. What does it mean? I'd written the boner off to some weird adrenaline, but now it's a possibility that it was something else entirely. There's a chance that I understand him a little better, the kinds of things that get him going, and it's kind of blowing my perception of him to pieces.

Dick and hand necklaces.

I have to smother a laugh as Baby keeps talking.

∞∞∞

Class is somehow wilder than Baby described. They've stuck to the classroom theme to the point of almost overdoing it, but it's the amount of people here that makes it feel intense. I've been here ten minutes, if even, and have been clipped by an elbow on all sides. After the shit Cade put me through today, I'm having a hard time not letting each hit—accidental or not—get to me. I honestly regret coming. I'm not even sure why I did.

Cade. I know it had something to do with him, but now that I'm here—heart pounding a little too hard, sweat making my shirt cling uncomfortably to my skin, and hackles rising the tiniest bit every time I'm touched by some stranger—I know that it wasn't worth it. Maybe I wanted to mess with him, show him that I couldn't be ignored, but right now, that doesn't sound so bad.

If anything, he's the one with all the power here. Annoying me by just existing. Went from pressing his boner against me to staying away from me—always in my line of sight, but not close enough to touch.

When Baby hands me a shot, I can't decide if I want to take it or not. It could be nice. Maybe. But I'm on meds that it wouldn't mix well with, and I'm trying to be better about things like this. It's awkward, though, admitting you're a twenty-one-year-old college kid who doesn't drink, so I do take it in my hand—hold it for a bit like a moron.

I just want to fit in, I guess, even if it makes me a little sick to my stomach just to be here, to have this shot glass in my hand. Cade makes it worse, of course. He downs his shot quickly, seems to swallow it without a second thought.

It hits me, for fuck knows how many times at this point, just how easy things are for him. I force myself not to fixate on him, follow his lead, and keep my attention on anything but him.

My new resolve only lasts a few minutes, though. Baby lost interest in me when his attempts at conversation fell flat, and he's made friends with a few others and is busy dancing with them. So my eyes find Cade once again. And then again.

A part of me had assumed that he was some kind of interested in men as the night progressed because why else would he be here? Plus, with the whole hard-dick-against-my-thigh thing earlier, it just makes sense that he would be some shade on the rainbow. But seeing it is something else entirely.

Cade is an aggressive flirt. Handsy as fuck. The kind of ballsy that would have me balking, but for whatever reason has the few guys he's moved through tonight going putty in his hands. I can see how he'd be considered hot enough to get away with it, but it's still strange to see so many guys enjoy it. And he always ends up moving on, leaving them either pissed or confused, even though each one of them has clearly been interested in more.

He's a bit slutty with it, to be honest. An attention whore, maybe. A fucking tease at the very least. I can't look away.

And Baby's stick-together rule means that I get to witness all of it. Like right now, I have a front-row seat as Cade slips his hand over some twink's navel, his mouth moving against the guy's ear as Cade whispers something that has his eyes fluttering shut. What the fuck could he be saying that would warrant *that* reaction?

I don't know, but thinking about it has my whole body tensing. I'm on the dance floor, barely moving because he keeps distracting me. It feels like my skin is vibrating, uneasiness clawing at every inch of me. The shot glass is still in my hand, being held with my fingertips as I hide it at my side. It might be empty by now, with as many times as I've been jostled. I'm about to check when a hand slaps heavily on my shoulder, and I drop the thing altogether.

"Hey there!"

I have to turn to see who it is, shooting them a glare because I'm in a mood, and that greeting fucking sucked. He's a fairly built guy with a broad grin to match that broad chest of his. The type I usually go for—someone easily matched with me—and my dirty look doesn't even throw him off, so I know he can handle a little attitude. He kind of reminds me of Cade, only his goofy smile is actually pointed at me.

Cade doesn't smile at me like this—not ever. His grins are usually self-assured, the kind that makes me want to slap it off his face—not at all like the smiles he's wearing tonight. Those smiles are like gay-guy magnets, has all kinds of men flocking to him. But they're not pointed at me.

Actually, now that I've had a second to look, they don't really look alike. This guy is a brunette. That's their only similarity, so I'm a little bothered that I compared them at all. Thoughts of Cade are infesting my mind, making it so that every single thing I see has me finding some connection to him. It's gross.

I lean in close to hear what the stranger says and only catch it at the end as he asks if I want to go sit down. I do want that. I very much want that and am nodding my head and moving off the dancefloor as soon as he finishes asking.

I shoot a glance over my shoulder, looking for Baby to tell him I'm moving, but I find Cade instead. He's watching me, doesn't even bother looking away as I catch him in the act. He still has his hands on the guy from earlier, the one currently grinding himself all over Cade. Not that he seems to notice, his eyes too busy glowering at me to give the poor dude any attention.

It has my stomach tightening, an awareness sweeping over me in a way that makes me feel one of those pesky emotions mixed with smugness again. This time, instead of guilt, it's something close to satisfaction. It shouldn't be as annoying as it is, but if anyone could make satisfaction something negative, I suppose it would be Cade.

But still. The restlessness I was suffering is settling into something much more comfortable, a low hum rather than the violent thrumming from before. It makes me feel like I have the upper hand, me being the one who caught *him* in a pissy mood over *me*. Especially knowing he's ignoring the person who is *still* all over him. I don't know why he's glaring and refusing to look away, but I like it. It's enlivening, in a way. Like maybe I wanted his attention on me all along. It has my mood perking up, a physical smile and a mental middle finger pointed his way.

Seems only fair, honestly. It was feeling frustratingly one-sided, this gross compulsion to just look at him. I let him see the cocky grin on my face before turning away from him and following this random guy off the floor.

"So, I thought I'd rescue you."

"Huh?" I didn't catch anything he just said, and the

laugh he lets out tells me he knows it.

"I was saying you looked lonely out there. Seemed like you needed a friend." He shrugs, his mouth pulled in that crooked grin that doesn't seem to waver. When I don't say anything, he tries again. "So, you come here often?"

I chuckle, more out of politeness than anything at the lame joke. I wouldn't usually bother, but I'm still riding the high that came with pissing off Cade, and it's partly thanks to this guy. "First time."

"Yeah? That's cool. Any chance you want to hit detention?"

I let out a full-on laugh at that, have to. "No thanks." Baby told me that it was a barely lit room filled with horny guys getting each other off, and unless I was down with that, I should say no to detention invites. The Zoloft kind of kills most of my sex drive anyway. "Not my thing."

"Ah." He nods, still grinning, obviously not too miffed at the rejection.

"What's your name?" I ask when he doesn't show signs of moving on to someone else.

"Corby." He holds his hand up when my smile grows. "It's the name I was given, man, I don't know."

"I'm Nic."

It's kind of crazy how much one little glare from Cade cheered me up. I'm able to comfortably chat with this guy—no pressure to impress since I've already turned him down, and on most days, it would be much harder. I'm good with people, but only when I try—and it's rare that I'm in the mood to try. Right now, though, it's relatively painless.

It doesn't hurt that we have some things in common. I find out he goes to the same college I'll be going to, studying psychology—the field I'm interested in. He says it's possible we'll see each other —likely be in a class or two together, and I think I'd be okay with that.

When he orders drinks, I don't want to decline. I take my meds in the mornings anyway. I doubt it'll hit me too hard now. It's not like I make a habit of it. And if I start feeling too dizzy, I can stop.

"Do you have a boyfriend?" he asks as we're finishing up our third drink. Or, I am, anyway. I don't know how many he's had, but it's clearly more than me.

"No," I answer easily, though I'm a little worried he maybe isn't taking the rejection as well as I'd thought. Maybe Corby being drunk has him forgetting, or at least desperate enough to try again. I hope not. I don't really have friends—and Baby is nice, but I don't want Cade's friends. Part of me moving forward, the plan my therapist and I worked on, included making an effort to make *connections*. That's the word she used, claiming that I haven't made any meaningful ones since I was much younger.

"Why not? Can't manage to convince anyone to put up with you?"

"You're projecting." I roll my eyes, keeping things light by joking along with him. "I could have had you, remember?"

"Yeah, well, I'm desperate." He shrugs. "Before

I came along, you were standing there all alone. Looking sad."

"Pfft." I wave a hand, physically sweeping that thought away. If I were being honest, I might actually agree with that, but right now, I'm feeling buzzed. Not sad. "I could have anyone I want."

This time, it's him who rolls his eyes.

"I could!" I insist. "Anyone."

"Wanna bet? Say, fifty bucks?" He swallows the rest of his drink and smiles at me as he places his ice-filled cup back on the table.

"Well, I'm not looking for—"

"That's what I thought!" he cuts me off, laughing a little and annoying me enough that I bristle.

"I'm just not in the mood for any of that right now."

"Says the guy who can't get none."

"That's a double negative," I grumble, but he's too drunk to understand the grammar policing right now. "What if—" I sigh. "I'll just get someone's phone number. Then you owe me fifty bucks."

"I get to pick the person," he says way too animatedly, but I shrug. Whatever. I've never had a problem *getting some* when I want it—it's just been a while since I have. "A phone number is too easy, though. You have to kiss them."

That has my spirits sinking. I don't do that—for reasons I'm not willing to dive into at the moment, but I don't want to explain that to this guy I just met. Kissing is... not something I can do.

I think about it for a moment—just a few seconds

too long—before deciding that I'm buzzed enough that maybe a simple kiss won't bother me too much, and then I'm agreeing to this bullshit bet. A peck. I can handle that.

He holds his hand out, and I roll my eyes as I shake it. When he points—with a smile that tells me he clearly thinks I'm going to strike out—I turn around and find the stranger he wants me to smooch.

"Alright." Of course, the guy he points to is standing pretty close to the one person in the massive crowd who hates me. He's even glaring at me as I stand up, still hanging by Baby but much closer to the bar now. He's not as brave this time around and looks away quickly, but I have a feeling he'll look again, and that thought pushes my feet across the room.

Just a kiss. Possibly while Cade watches me. I can do this. I kind of hate spit, the feel of a tongue on mine makes me gag. It's why I usually avoid kissing altogether

"Hi!" I speak loudly, having to lean in close to a guy just about my size. I have no game, but I'm drunk and could use fifty bucks—and really want to annoy Cade —so I utter a simple, "Want to kiss me?" and hope it works.

It does. The guy is attractive, darker skinned with dreads that fall forward and skim my cheek when he leans in to lay one on me. His lips are warm as they cover mine, instantly taking complete control of the kiss. It makes me nervous and has me stiffening up in anticipation of a tongue. My palms only just touch his chest to push him when I feel myself being tugged away from behind.

"He's too drunk!"

It's fucking Cade, yelling at the random dude who just won me fifty dollars for no reason. I'm almost grateful because I was just about to push him off of me, but mostly, I'm petty and annoyed that he's stepping in.

"What the fuck, Cade?"

"You're shitfaced—we gotta go."

"No! We—" But the guy is gone. I give Cade a glare, but see Corby walking up behind him.

Corby—which I've decided is a stupid ass name—just laughs as shoves his way past my stupid ass roommate. "Did you lie, Nic—do you actually have a boyfriend?"

"He's my stepbrother." I leave it at that, letting it explain both questions.

His brows jump to his hairline, mild shock still on his face as he starts talking. "Stepbrothers count as anyone too, y'know? Fifty more bucks, and—"

"Absolutely not."

He laughs into his cup, which definitely doesn't have anything but melted ice in it by now. "It would be pretty hot, though. And he looked crazy jealous just now."

"No, it isn't. And he was not."

"It is, and yes, he was."

"The game is over!" I yell. "You lose. Pay up, sucka."

"Mm, alright, I guess." He reaches into his pocket to grab his wallet, finally giving me my money. "But that sucks for you because he's hot."

I ignore that last part and look over his shoulder to see Cade glaring at me as Baby hangs off his arm. Cade has always been someone I know is attractive, and I guess he is pretty close in looks to the guys I've been with. Guys kind of like Corby, but both he and my stepbrother are annoying.

Cade is still glaring at me as Corby tells me I should hit him up sometime, and I can't explain how happy it makes me. The kiss didn't make him jealous, but it did piss him off for some reason, and I'm all about that.

Six

Cade

"What's wrong with you?"

We've been back long enough, and I mean, he definitely had a few, but he shouldn't still be wasted.

"Nic."

"Shut the fuck up, Cade." He sighs, finally moving away from the bathroom door where he's been standing for the past minute. He's not moving normally, though.

My mouth opens and then closes just as quickly so I can—smartly—swallow the words I feel compelled to say. He doesn't want me checking in on him, and I'm not even sure why I want to. But he's walking so slowly and a little wobbly. It's making me uneasy. He has a history of being... not okay.

"Are you drunk?" I make myself ask for peace of mind. "How much *did* you drink?" I couldn't help but notice him and his buddy—whoever the fuck that guy was—sitting together. Like friends. I've never known

Nic to have friends. Plus, the guy looked like a tool. Kind of skeevy. Maybe he drugged him. Maybe that's why Nic kissed that fucker.

"I'm... dizzy. Or something."

"Dizzy." I scoff, my fingertips pulling at the fabric of the shorts I changed into when we got back. "Lightweight." I don't sound as easygoing as I mean to.

"I'm not a lightweight." He scowls at me, and for whatever reason, the sight of it makes me feel better, my chest less tight. It's almost normal—like he's close to himself. But still, it seems like something isn't right.

"Coulda fooled me."

"It's just my leg, and... I'm really tired and still buzzed. I'm fine. Just need to lie down." But he doesn't lay down. He just sits there with his eyes closed, bracing himself with his hands on the bed.

I want to tell him that he should be careful, that if drinking makes him walk like a baby deer, then maybe he shouldn't drink. But I don't think me showing any actual concern for him would go over well.

Plus, I don't have any actual concern for the guy. He can do whatever he wants—put himself into alcohol poisoning for all I care. But then I look at him and instantly change my mind.

"You're bleeding." I stand up, my body pushing me to act, but I get stuck as soon as I'm off the bed. It takes him a second, confusion flooding his features before the blood trickles over his lip enough that he finally feels it.

"Shit," he mumbles, his hand cupping his nose to

catch what he can.

"Are you… good?"

"It's just the ibuprofen."

"I—what? That makes no sense." I finally move and pick up the shirt I left on my bed before we all left for Class. When I give it to him, he doesn't hesitate to hold it against his face.

"My meds—they don't react well together."

"What meds?"

"None of your business." He shoots me an indignant look, but with my tee, all wadded up under his nose, it doesn't have the effect I'm sure he's going for.

It's true. It's none of my business, but also, he's my roommate. So, maybe it should be my business. I'm forced to spend an unfortunate amount of time with the prick, so I should know these things. Right? At the very least, so I'm prepared for stuff like this.

"Does this happen a lot?"

Another glare.

"What meds? How much did you drink? I don't think—"

"Cadence. Fuck off."

"No." I move back and sit down on the edge of my bed to make a point. "It's my room."

He scoffs—I swear we could have entire conversations consisting of that one little sound at this point—and my lips try to pull into another smile, but I stop them. The urge is gone when he moves to stand up. I make sure to beat him to it because just what the hell does he think he's doing?

"Sit down. Nic, *stop*," I order, my hands on his shoulders to keep him from trying again. "Don't be stupid."

He goes quiet—or *stays* quiet, I guess—and it takes a few seconds of that to recognize that I'm being weird. I can't even think of a time I've ever touched him. Hit him, pushed at him, elbowed him—stuff like that has happened a lot. This is none of those.

I remove my hands and let them fall to my sides, where they feel strange. Almost heavy. "You should sit down." Which he's already doing. *Idiot.* "You're dizzy. And bleeding."

"I need to wash my face."

"Well... wait." I step away, moving into the bathroom with what feels like choppy movements. I pull a hand towel off the rack and wait for the sink water to start running warm before wetting it. I move fast, specifically not letting myself think about things too closely, and am back in front of him not even a minute later. "Here." I hold the damp towel out, reaching for my shirt with my free hand while doing so.

But he's Nic, and nothing with him is easy, so he ends up stubbornly leaning back enough that I can't reach it. "Stop mother henning me. I swear, you're just like your mom—so fucking annoying."

"At least I'm not like *your* mom."

My whole body tenses as I wait, locking up like I expect him to strike. I regret saying it pretty instantaneously, a bit guilty even. She's *not well.* That's the only actual information my mom ever gave me. I don't know what his relationship with that woman is, but I do know that he's very protective of her, and I probably should not have said that shit.

But he doesn't react. Not really. He stares at me, his grey eyes narrowed a bit, but other than that... nothing.

It's underwhelming. My shoulders slump like I'm some kind of letdown, but that can't be. It's a *relief* that he's not putting his hands on me, not a disappointment. When he finally moves—reaches a hand out—I flinch. Just a little—the tiniest bit, really—but it's a degrading move all the same. He grabs the wet cloth out of my hand, and then it's even worse. I overreacted. He was *not* about to choke me.

"I'm not going to reward you for your poor behavior, Cade."

"Wha—" I sputter, the question tripping on its way out. "What the hell is that supposed to mean?" But my face heats as he cocks that judgemental bicolored brow at me. We both know what it means.

Maybe—*I hope*—I'm wrong, but there's something in the look he gives me that tells me he sees right through me.

I take a few steps backward and wordlessly sit on my bed, feeling out of place in the room I've slept in for the past couple of years because my room is also Nic's now.

"Are you okay?" I make myself ask in an effort to change the subject. But also, I need the peace of mind. Assholery aside, I want him to be okay.

Because if he weren't, it'd be a hassle. A heap of

unnecessary stress. He'd be a bigger pain in the ass than he already is. That's all this compulsive need to *mother hen* him is.

Nic wipes at his face with the towel, not looking at me as he does it. When he finally meets my gaze, I have to make myself hold his stare and ignore the smeared blood above his mouth. Just when I think he's going to ignore me, he gives me a nod, and I take a very slow breath, relieved. He's okay, and there's no problem.

I gotta watch him, it seems. Maybe find out what meds he's on so I can read up on it. It'd be good to know, I think. But, for now, he's okay.

This time, when he gets up to go to the bathroom, I let him.

It gives me time to consider the bullshit he just said. I know what he meant, but... well, what the fuck did he mean? Like his hands anywhere on me is some prize. *Reward.* Pfft.

∞ ∞ ∞

A sharp exhale has me holding still the second I wrap my hand around my dick. After a swift look to make sure that Nic is still asleep, I slide my fist up in one long, achingly slow stroke that is not at all relieving—because, of course, it's not.

My hand is dry, and *he* is only a few feet away. I can

hear him breathing, making it too hard to settle into the right mindset for this.

But I *need* it. Something has got to give. I'm embarrassing myself at this point. It's been too long since I've done this or had any sort of release—before he showed up, I'm pretty sure. And if someone like Nic is getting to me, it's a must that I get it over with.

I drag my hand out from under the covers and lick my palm in one long stripe, hoping that it's enough to get past the initial discomfort. It takes longer than it should since I'm forced to move slowly and keep quiet so I don't wake him up.

I don't even know what I'd do if Nic did wake up. *Fuck.* That'd be humiliating.

My head leans back, sinks into my pillow as I roll my lips between my teeth to keep a moan from escaping. I can feel my frustrations uncoiling that much more with every new muscle that pulls tight. My palm skims over my slit, collecting precum to make the glide easier. Each stroke laps at my spine until it's hard to keep my breaths quiet, and I have to look to make sure Nic is still asleep.

He's facing the wall, the white patch of hair on the back of his head visible in the little bit of moonlight that seeps through our curtains. Still sleeping.

"*Fuck.*" I make myself look away, but tearing my eyes off of him doesn't convince me that I'm not being a pervert right now. I shouldn't be doing this. Not right here, with Nic right there. *I should stop.* It feels wrong.

A quiet moan should have me freezing, but I find

myself chasing more instead. My hips jerk, a shallow fuck up into my fist that makes my stomach clench. I know I should stop, but it's too good. Nic could wake up at any second, but it's *so* fucking good.

My free hand finds its way to my neck, and I can't even pretend I don't want it there. I let it rest, a loose band that has a shiver raking across my skin. I don't understand why it feels so nice—it's barely even a tease. But the soft touch gives me a sense of craving that's vibrating beneath my skin, slowly building into something overwhelming. My hand starts to tighten —both of them do. *Oh, god.* I need a little more. *More.*

"*Cade.*"

"Fu—" I gasp, my body stuttering to a stop. "*Fuck.*"

"What are you doing?"

"Nothing. I—nothing." The hand still wrapped around my cock squeezes, and I let go quickly with a hiss.

"Nothing," his sleep-rumpled voice parrots. He sounds pissed. Annoyed, maybe, at having been woken up. That's all it is. No way he knows what—"You're over there moaning like you're getting paid for it, but sure. Let's go with *nothing.*"

"Fuck you," I spit, face heating. "That's—"

A bitter little chuckle has me shutting up, face on fire, and pulse racing. I was on the verge of coming, all sorts of feel-good shit coursing through me, and it's all gone. Poof. Just like that. Chased away by that cocky laugh.

"Pretty sure it's you who needs to be fucked, little brother."

My cock jumps, raises up off my abs, heavy and hard enough to move the blanket a bit. So maybe that feel-good shit isn't completely gone—still there and getting all mixed up in this confusing little bubble of humiliation.

"What the fuck is wrong with you?" My head shakes, refusing to admit fault here. Shit like this happens. Like Liam and I never heard each other? Of course, we did. "A normal person would have ignored it," I insist, like somehow pointing this out will shift the blame off of me.

"A normal person wouldn't be fucking his fist a few feet away from his big brother."

I know he's only trying to goad me, to piss me off, and I fucking hate that it works. He doesn't think of me as family and never has.

"You're *not* my brother. You're just the baggage me and my mom got stuck with." I'm back to breathing heavy, pissed off in a way that only Nicolas Aldana can bring on. There are too many things going on right now, and my body doesn't know how to react. My dumb dick is still hard. It aches. I can feel it throbbing, and it's difficult to ignore.

"Are you imagining it's mine?"

"*What?*" I scoff, turning to see him through the dark room. Nothing about Nic makes sense. "What the fuck are you—"

"The hand on your throat."

My fingers flex against my pulse point, the rest of me unmoving as a breath gets caught in my chest. I forgot it was there.

"If you are, you need to squeeze tighter."

"Shut up." My eyes screw tight, my embarrassment nearing the point of smothering.

"If it were mine, you wouldn't even be able to speak. Breathe."

"Shut up," I plead, my voice annoyingly whiny as my hand stays right where it is.

"God, listen to you."

But I'm listening to *him*, to the gravel still lacing his words—the sound of them rumbling in the space between us. Rough and coarse—it's doing shit to me. I hate it.

"Are you embarrassed? You fucking should be, Cade." He lets out another dark laugh that has my skin crawling, every inch of me begging for relief. What's wrong with me? I *am* embarrassed, but it's like my cock hasn't gotten the message. Still stiff, almost in pain, and for what? Not Nic, with all this venom in his voice. There's no way.

"You could have..." I take a breath, try to calm down. "Ignored me."

"Yeah, but that's not what you wanted, is it?"

I don't speak. It feels like a rhetorical question, but also, I'm not sure I know the answer.

"Those moans, they're not that quiet, Cade. You wanted me to know. You like my hand so much—such a pathetic little slut for it—that you couldn't help yourself, huh?" His breath hitches, and I can't even begin to describe the instant relief that sound gives me, the feeling of it overpowering the shock at his words.

"Are you—" A sound a lot like a moan drowns out my question as I take myself in hand once again. I don't have to worry about a dry stroke this time—my dumb dick is drooling, doesn't understand how wrong this is.

Or, hell. Maybe it does. Maybe that's why it's acting like this, has *me* acting like this. *A pathetic little slut.* Another moan, softer now, makes me roll my face into my pillow in the hopes that I can smother the sound.

But his bed is so close. He can definitely hear everything I'm doing, and I'm too keyed up to mind it. I have no intention of stopping. God, I don't even think I could.

There's an absolutely demented part of me that wants him to keep talking. Say it again, say more. I need him to keep talking.

"You are so desperate for my attention, practically begging for it."

"*Oh, god.*" My back bows, nothing muffling the needy sounds coming out of my mouth now.

The quiet laugh he lets out is cruel, has anticipation coiling around my balls as they pull up in a tight hug against the base of my dick. "You like this," he says. "You *want* to be degraded by me. That's cute, little brother."

"*Nic,*" I groan, the protest dissolving as my hand moves faster, fist squeezing tighter. Slick sounds barely audible as I fuck my fist, just like he said.

"That's right," he agrees, almost like a praise, and the sound of it pushes me closer. "I'm not even touching you, but it's me making you feel this good.

Say it again."

It's disgusting how fast I listen. "*Nic*. Fuck." My hips lift off the bed, meeting a downward stroke as the air is expelled from my lungs, my vision whiting out as bliss barrels through me. A grunt trips over a whine as I try to smother the sounds of my orgasm, but as I stroke myself through it, everything gets wet—every stroke making noise as I drag my cum up and down my cock.

It's not until my body finally slumps that I feel the beginnings of regret.

That did not take very long at all—coming for Nic. Not once I got started anyway. How am I going to live that down? I don't know how to move on from this. How to explain it.

I blame my dumb dick. Have to.

But I mean... it felt good. Still kind of does, even with shame trying to ruin it. My hand caught most of my cum, which is quickly cooling as I softly stroke through the aftershocks with a loose grip, and the soft grunt I let out has me finally letting go of my neck. My stomach twitches through the comedown as I catch my breath, feeling a little cold now that I'm not chasing the orgasm I so desperately needed.

I feel oddly settled. At ease. As my heart starts to pump slower, I get the crazy thought that the comedown is almost better than the orgasm. It just feels so good, so peaceful. Pretty foreign. I can't even remember the last time I felt so relaxed.

And then I remember Nic.

I'm being loud, breaths so heavy that I can't even

hear him. For a moment, a very quick second, I thought he was touching himself. I heard it in his voice—in the words that had me overwhelmingly turned on—and I was excited because it meant that I wasn't alone. I wasn't the only brainless one in the room. But I'm less sure now.

"Did you..." God, he just listened to me come. Talked me through it. Why is it so awful to ask? I really don't see how it can get any worse—unless he didn't. Wasn't into it like I was. I mean, fuck. I was *into it*.

He came. The alternative is that he meant the things he said. He called me things that only work if he was getting something out of it too. I don't know what this was, but I know that I want him to say yes. Yes, he was touching himself. Yes, he finished. Yes, he fucking liked it. *Just say yes, asshole.*

"No." He scoffs.

"Bullshit," I call his bluff as my stomach drops. "You were—"

"I think it's obvious you have a little crush on me, but let's not get it twisted. That shit is one-sided, Cade. I can barely even stand to look at you—nothing about you makes my dick hard."

"That's—" It hurts my feelings, which is ridiculous. I shake my head, searching for the right thing to say—something that *doesn't* make me look stupid. I have to blink as my eyes start to water. "I don't have a crush on you. And I am *not* a slut."

I think I might have made myself look stupid anyway.

He laughs, not nearly as sexy-sounding as he had

been only minutes prior, and it has me sitting up.

"All that cum on you kind of says otherwise."

I regret existing at this point. My dumb dick has moved past dumb. That thing is the stupidest fucking... it... "You're so... you—"

He chuckles darkly, all smug with it, and I wish I were anywhere but here. "You should clean yourself up."

What a loser. I am such a loser.

"Fuck you," I spit, but I'm on my feet, Dumb Dick all tucked away in my boxers, because, yeah. I do need to clean myself up.

Seven

Nic

I consider it. Jerking off. My cock is demanding attention, aching. But it would take too long. That's... well, I can't do that. He came ridiculously fast, was close that whole time. That's the norm for guys our age. It's not like that for me—that easy. It hasn't been for a while.

Everything I've read—*read* because it's too daunting to ask a professional outright—says it'll only be a problem until I stop taking my antidepressants. Usually, it's only a mild concern. Being turned on and wanting sex don't always go hand in hand with me. In fact, it's sort of out of the ordinary for that to happen. Looking for sex really means that I'm looking for a break. A way to punish myself. It's never all that nice or comforting. I say yes, but I can't say I've ever actually wanted it. It's simply what I need in those moments. Deserve.

Right now, though, I can't imagine putting myself through that. I want... something. Not to hurt, and isn't that something? That I want to feel *good*.

How irritating that it's because of Cade.

But the last thing I need is for Cade to witness me struggling to come. I'd never live that down. Hell, I don't know how he's going to live what just happened down. I chuckle at the thought. How embarrassing for him. That he gave in so easily, enjoyed me and my general disdain for him so much. The sounds he made...

I groan, giving myself a single stroke before I let go completely. It's not a good idea. But neither was that whole mess.

I shouldn't have done it. Spoken to him like that. Everything I've done in regard to him since I showed up here has been wrong. It's like I walked into a mess and just started wiping it down, but instead of cleaning shit up, it's only spread it all around. Made things worse. I don't like hearing things like that—the things I said to him.

I feel guilty. It's sitting heavy in my stomach. But it's also not killing the urge to come, and that makes me feel even worse. I shouldn't have done it, and I definitely shouldn't have liked it.

Cade wasn't wrong in saying that I could have ignored it. That's what I should have done. Instead, I told him to say my name. I wanted to hear it—those sexy moans all wrapped in *my name* because it was me who caused them. It was presumptuous and bold, but I knew I was right.

He was touching himself because of me—the stepbrother he hates. He knew it. He might have even hated it but was too weak to deny himself. He wanted it—*me*—too badly.

It was kind of nice not being the weak one for once. That in itself is good enough to negate the blue balls. Or that's what I try to convince myself anyway. The way the fabric of my sweats stretches over my dick as I move tells me it doesn't exactly agree. I can't remember the last time it had been so needy, so hard. It's like it's been dormant, this side of me. I guess all it needed was for me to call a guy a slut.

Too bad it's a waste.

My shoulders relax as I make my way into the hallway. I need more of that, that easy breathing and muscle relief—a lot more of it—before I go back in there.

It's hard to believe someone like Cade wants me that way. I was there and still can't seem to wrap my head around it.

"*Hey*," a hushed voice startles me, making me jump.

"What the fuck?"

"Sorry," Baby says with a little snicker. "What are you doing?"

I stand there, feeling strange as my cock slowly softens in this dark hallway. Hopefully, he can't see it. "I can't sleep."

He hums, still standing there in front of his door. "Want to smoke a bowl? Helps me sleep sometimes." His slim shoulders shrug, visible even in the dark.

Baby's alright. He's... snarky? Mostly nice. Unless he's talking to Logan. I've only seen him a handful of times, but each time involved Baby snapping at him.

"Sure," I say just before my silence gets awkward. "But don't bite me."

He laughs at that like I'm kidding. But I'm not. I don't want to be high and have him chomp on me out of nowhere.

"Do you like it here?" he asks me as he opens his door.

I have to squint to filter the sudden light and end up closing my eyes altogether as I get closer. "Um, yeah. It's cool."

"What's it—you can sit on the bed. Or the bean bag. What's it like rooming with Cade?"

It's still hard to open my eyes, not used to the light just yet, but I manage to pry them open enough to see the massive bean bag chair he has sitting in the corner of his room. This room is a lot smaller than the one Cade and I share, but this chair is huge.

"It's... fine," I say as I sit back, the top of my shoulders leaning back against the wall. What a loaded question. It sucks. Cade in my face close to twenty-four-seven is frustrating, but also, it's not half as bad as I thought it was going to be.

"He's cool. I like to tease him, but he's pretty much always been my favorite roommate."

"You didn't like Liam?"

"Everybody likes Liam. It's hard not to."

I bristle at that. I personally found it real easy. He and Cade have always been the very definition of unlikeable in my eyes.

"Plus, I mean——" He pauses to take the first hit,

cornering the edge of the bowl with his pink lighter. I honestly expected more pink in here, but looking around, it's very muted. Even this fat bean bag chair is a basic grey. The most color is on his bed, a cluster of stuffed animals all over his pillows, which makes sense. It's not that Baby is all that femme— the occasional crop top and girly pajamas—but he just seemed frilly. I expected more pink.

It feels like a small forever before he's talking again. "He's hot."

I scoff, taking the pipe from his outstretched hand as he settles crisscross on the edge of his bed.

"Are you gonna try to lie and say he's not?"

"He's…" I grunt, choosing to inhale rather than answer. He's alright. Anytime I saw him, he was next to Cade, so I'm sure that has something to do with why I've never been impressed. It'd be hard for anyone to stand out next to Cade.

"He's hot. So is his boyfriend."

I cough. I cough *loudly*, my lungs burning at the failed attempt that sad hit was. "*Fuck*," I wheeze, my chest burning. "Holy shit." I drag in a deep breath as Baby lets out another one of those creepy little laughs.

"You good?"

"Fine. I just thought… what did you say?" I blink away the moisture in my eyes and ignore the pinch in my lung.

"What?" He takes his weed back.

I try to clear my throat again, ignoring it when Baby laughs at me.

"Are you a lightweight? Want to skip a few?"

I glare at him as I hold my hand out. That's the second time I've been called that in the span of a few hours. "I'm not a big pothead, so excuse me for choking on literal smoke." Shithead. "You were talking about Liam and..." I wave a hand, holding my breath and hoping he can't tell that I'm holding in another bark.

"Oh, yeah. Homie just decided he was into dudes one day and bagged the hottest, beefiest, tattooed gay man in the city. *Sebastian.*"

"*Liam*—Cade's best friend?" I ask, hoping to make sense of this shit. Maybe I am a lightweight. Two hits might be enough for me. "I thought he was a homophobe."

He laughs, *loudly.* "So did I! When I first met him, I'd flirt with him relentlessly. I was trying to press his buttons but I don't know. I don't think he realized that's what I was doing—he's not exactly the sharpest tool in the shed. Poor thing." He smiles like one might grin when talking about a baby or something. "At least he's pretty."

"He's not—whatever." I huff, leaning back with a flick of my wrist when he tries to hand it back to me. Liam and Cade always had girls all over them, but it's possible my bias has kept me from seeing them as anything more than annoying as fuck. They both like men now. Nothing makes sense. I'm cutting myself off.

"He has a boyfriend?"

"Mmhm. A big one."

I sink lower in the chair—why do they call bean bag

chairs chairs? It's not a chair. It's a bag. There are no legs. But it is nice to sit on. I stretch my neck over the back of it, getting comfortable. It feels like my head is floating and like I need something to drink, but it's also just peaceful, and I don't want to get up.

"A big one." I huff a quiet laugh out of my nose. "Wait. Does Cade know?" That's a dumb question. They're best friends. They know everything about each other.

Baby's eyes widen as he nods, excited to speak but not wanting to waste the hit he just took. "Yup." The *p* pops on his lips. "He kissed Liam."

"That's not surprising." It's really not—Cade has always been a little too obsessed with the baseball player. I close my eyes and ignore it when I feel a bit of *something* in my chest. Not just weed.

"No, you don't get it. Liam was dating Sebastian already. Like, head over heels for the guy, and Cade kissed him anyway."

I open one eye. "What?" That's fucked up, but also, I'm not surprised.

Baby nods. "Got sent to the hospital for it."

"*What?*" I sit up, but that kind of sucks, so I let myself fall back immediately.

He goes on to tell me a whole lot of stuff that makes fuck all sense. Liam likes a dick, and that dick punched Cade in the face—*broke* his nose. I don't get it. They've been best friends since... well, I don't even know. Long before I came into the picture. Why would Liam be okay with that—with his supposed boyfriend hitting his best friend?

What a bitch. Both of them—Liam and the tattooed beefy dude. I don't even like Cade, and it bugs me that someone hit him.

Someone *else*.

That's got to be why I haven't seen Liam around. A part of me wondered, but mostly, I was relieved. Cade is a lot more tolerable on his own. They used to do everything together.

Liking dick is included in that *everything*, apparently.

"He's coming over tomorrow. Today, I guess."

"Oh." I get to watch Cade get all dopey around him again. "Wonderful."

∞ ∞ ∞

"**W**hat the fuck?"

I pause rubbing my eyes, and shut Baby's door as quietly as I can. He's still asleep. It's just instinct to try and keep quiet, not be a rude fuck. That's, of course, not in Cade's instincts, though.

"You slept in Baby's room."

It doesn't sound like a question, and if it were, it'd be too stupid to answer anyway. Because obviously, I did. I didn't mean to, but he—my now favorite roommate—was right. Weed can knock a lightweight out. And bean bag chairs are cozy as fuck.

"Why?"

I look at him, fresh-faced and bright-eyed. It's too fucking early to look that good. Unless you're Cadence Howard, I guess. The backpack hanging at his side clues me in that he's dressed for school, so it's slightly forgivable. It'd be more so if he didn't look like a dweeb. He wears a lot of basic T-shirts. Plain. Most of my shirts are graphic band tees, something I remember him hating on when we were teens.

I wouldn't call Cade posh, but he's very much put together. Preppy is maybe a better word. Always has been. A lot like Liam, actually.

The reminder that Li is supposed to be here later today has my eyes narrowing. My thighs hurt, I'm dehydrated, and my eyes feel like they've been rubbed with sandpaper, so I'm in a bad mood and don't want to deal with this first thing in the morning. "Can you just tell me what your problem is so we can get it over with?"

"Why were you in Baby's room?" He's glaring, looking way too tense for a guy who had the privilege of coming his brains out last night.

That's why I was in Baby's room. I want to tell him, but it's too early to deal with his nonsense. Still, I can't help but smile, and that—for whatever reason—only seems to piss him off more.

He scoffs, sputtering in that way he does so often. "You—" His eyes slide to the door at my shoulder, and he sighs, the sound rough as he aggressively runs a hand up and down his face a few times before he just walks past me altogether.

That was anticlimactic, and where I know I should be relieved not to have to put him in his place when I haven't even had the chance to piss today, I sort of feel uneasy about it. I grunt as I dig the heel of my palm into my leg, trying to soothe the burn just as Cade shuts the front door behind him.

Maybe he doesn't want me to be friends with his friends. He never wanted me around Liam, so it tracks. It's not even like we are friends, Baby and me. All we did was smoke and talk about nothing—my vitiligo, work, Christmas, and school plans. Nothing meaningful.

But it had been nice—once we stopped talking about Liam. I don't have friends. Corby. Sort of. It's hard for me to *make connections*. That's kind of my whole schtick, but it felt like I was on my way to doing that very thing last night.

What a piece of shit for not being okay with that. Good enough to make his dick hard when nobody is around but not good enough for his friends.

Eight

Cade

"**W**hat's your problem?"

"I don't have one." Except I do, and it's obvious. And beyond bothersome. Especially when said problem is talking to me, sitting a little too fucking close to me.

I've always liked Baby. It'll be a goddamn shame if that has to end over something as insignificant as *Nic*.

My jaw tenses before I make myself relax, my chest expanding with a sigh I don't want to let out. I'm all mixed up over my stepbrother. I'm not even that surprised. Being so mind-numbingly stupid means that these kinds of things happen. I am the king of inappropriate crushes.

Crush doesn't feel like the right word. I don't know how to explain it. But I *feel* it, and it's awful. Nic.

Nic, Nic, Nic.

He's like a disease. A nasty infection. Venomous little shit. I gotta hope I can suck the poison out somehow—before it's too late.

But there's a part of me that kind of hopes Nic does it for me. Gets on his knees and just sucks it right out. Seems only fair, since he's the whole reason I'm over here suffering and shit.

"But really, Cade. What's wrong?" Baby shuffles in his seat—right next to me on the couch—and the genuine concern on his face has me feeling close to guilty. "Is it because Sebastian is coming over?"

Movie night, he said. I want to be mad at Sebastian, but it doesn't feel like I can be. I went years wanting to kiss Liam and decided that the perfect time to actually do it—be brave and get it over with—was right after he got himself a boyfriend. That's a punchable offense. So, no, I'm not mad at him. That doesn't mean I want him here, but whatever. There are bigger issues.

"No." I roll my eyes. That's all I do these days. I can't help it—everything is just *so* ridiculous.

"Well. Okay, then what?"

"Did you and Nic fuck?"

"What?" His eyebrows jump to his hairline, the movement making a stray strand slip over his eye. I'd be a little shocked too, if I wasn't so focused on the way his cheeks flush. Little dude looks guilty.

My eyes narrow.

"I beg your *finest* pardon? Cadence..."

I huff. "It's a yes or no question, Baby."

"No! God. No, you freak." He gives a single shake of his head. "Where the hell did that come from?"

"He spent the night in your room," I deadpan.

"So?" He stares at me, searching my face for an answer, and then gasps. The sound of it is so dramatic

I have to fight the urge to jump. "You're jealous!" A shit-eating grin warps his face as he clambers onto his knees, moving closer to me.

"Ew, no. That's not what this is," I lie. I don't even realize it's a lie until I say it. "Don't change the subject."

Jealousy is a nasty feeling, and I am very much acquainted with it. I've been stuck wallowing in it ever since Liam first laid eyes on Sebastian. It's an ugly, baseless thing that I have no right to feel.

But, *fuck*, am I feeling it.

Only it's far worse than usual. More confusing. This is fucking *Nic* we're talking about.

"I called it!" He is way too excited about this—downright giddy as he slaps at my shoulder. "You guys *did* kiss! You pervert. You're hooking up with your stepbrother." He cackles, and the obnoxious sound of it pushes me to stand. Has he always been this annoying? "You guys would make bank doing porn."

I do not have to take this.

"Wait!" He grabs onto my arm, and I jerk it out of his hold. "No, I'll stop. I'm sorry." He pats the couch cushion, wanting me to sit back down, but I ignore him. "Sorry. If it helps, I don't think anyone would blame you." He shrugs. "Nic is crazy hot."

My brows dip at that. "Did you—"

"I already said no, dipshit. We just smoked a bit and passed out. He slept on my bean bag chair."

That's… mostly believable. I've slept on that thing a few times. I still squint at him, though. Maybe a tiny bit accusingly.

"Awe. Little jelly bean." He pokes at my stomach,

and I scoff.

"I'm not jealous—and we're not hooking up!"

"You are so—"

A key in the front door has both of us shutting up.

The vibe in the room as soon as Nic enters can only be described as uncomfortable. I have to hope that it's me alone experiencing it, but somehow, I doubt it. It's too charged—makes my skin crawl. No way is it just me.

It's absurd. All he did was walk in—looking like his sexy self—and it made me nervous. He doesn't speak to either of us, barely manages to give the room a clipped nod before he saunters off down the hall.

"Oof. I could *feel* the sexual tension," Baby says as soon as we hear my bedroom door shut.

"Eat a dick," I hiss.

"You know what... I just might. Gonna go see if Nicolas—"

"Sit the fuck down." I use one hand to *gently* push him back onto the couch when he tries to get up.

∞ ∞ ∞

Not even getting to pick the movie we all watch has me perking up. Liam and his giant boyfriend are cozied up on the loveseat while Logan somehow gets away with sitting next to Baby.

Nic is on the floor, not paying attention to the film as he scrolls through his phone.

And I'm just... here, feeling like I don't belong. Ignored.

I try not to focus on them, on anybody at all, but there's a low hum as they all talk quietly amongst themselves, and that feeling of being ignored starts to grow. It's been like this for months. I didn't realize how much I relied on Liam's friendship until I didn't have it anymore.

I know we said we were good, and things do seem that way for the most part, but things are different. He has his own life, and where that's always been the case, there's less room for me now that Sebastian is in the picture. I'm by myself a lot these days.

When I look over, I see Nic with his head craned as he talks to Sebastian of all people. They laugh and I clamp my mouth shut tight, jaw strained as I grind my teeth. I don't think I've ever seen either of them laugh. Assholes. Seems fitting that they'd get along.

I notice Liam shift closer to his boyfriend, practically on top of him at this point. When I look at him I catch him staring at me, a pissed-off look on his face. He thinks I was glaring at his precious *Bash*. I guess I was, but not for reasons he'd understand. Still, I fix my face and look back at the screen. How would he look at me if he knew the real reason I was staring?

Like I'd lost my mind. Have me hauled away and checked into some facility. It kind of feels necessary, to be honest. I could use an extended vacation locked up with some therapists.

I get up to grab a drink, and when I come back, I don't even think about it as I sit in front of the couch next to Nic. I want him to acknowledge me—I'd even settle for a glare, honestly. But he gives me nothing. Too busy ignoring me.

Well. That doesn't seem right. It's not fair. I shouldn't want him to notice me. But if not him, then who? Liam is busy. Baby and Logan are doing whatever they're doing, and I definitely do not want Sebastian's attention. Maybe I shouldn't want it to be Nic, but fuck. I want *somebody* to notice me.

So, I scoot over. Just a tad—no more than an inch—and when I feel his shoulders stiffen next to mine, I'm thrilled. The feeling zips through me and has my skin thrumming, my heart pumping a little harder.

"*Move.*"

I match his whisper with one of my own. "No."

He makes a sound close to a growl, quiet enough that only I can hear him, and it has my body comfortably slumping against the furniture behind us. It's almost relaxing, having things as they should be—Nic annoyed because of me and no longer talking to fucking Sebastian.

"Sit somewhere else."

"I'm fine here." My lips twitch when he huffs in response. *Consider it a punishment for making my dick hard.*

He doesn't pick his phone up again. Doesn't look over his shoulder to talk to the guy who broke my nose. He just sits here, right next to me, seething. I kind of love it.

It's uneventful, but it's... nice. My mind goes sort of blank as I pretend to watch the movie. There are a lot of things I could be worrying about. Liam. Finals are coming up. Going to my mom's for winter break. But somehow, Nic's attention is enough to have all my frazzled nerves settling. I sit there, mind at ease so long as his body stays stiff next to mine.

God, what's wrong with me?

This is not normal. It wasn't even twenty-four hours ago that the dude was calling me a slut.

My face heats, and my only saving grace at the moment is the credits that begin to roll on the TV. At least the room is mostly dark. But then Baby gets up and turns the light on, standing on his tiptoes as he stretches and I duck my head so nobody notices my frustration.

I don't pay attention to anything anybody says, too focused on the way Nic stays seated as the rest of the room starts to move about.

"Cade."

"Yeah? Oh." I blink, eyes meeting Sebastian's as he glares at me over Nic's head.

"I wanted to tell you..." He sighs, rolling his broad shoulders before trying again. "I'm—"

"Wait." I look for Liam who is coincidentally over by Baby, very unsubtly peeking over here every other split second. I understand what's going on instantly and wish I hadn't been so adamant that I needed to sit by Nic. Now he gets a front-row seat to this mess. "Let's not do this. I'm sorry, you don't need to be, and we're good."

His brows dip, that scowl he's always sporting deepening before he shrugs. "Yeah, I wish that was enough, but that's not going to satisfy my pr—Liam."

I snort. "It's not a real apology if you're only doing it because he wants you to."

"No, it's... I *am* sorry," he grumbles. "You deserved a punch, for sure."

"You're doing great so far." I give him a thumbs up with a small smile, teasing. "Solid apology."

"You did," he insists, ignoring my very poor attempts to make light of the situation. I know he's right, so I don't argue. "But I shouldn't have done... that. So, I'm sorry."

I'm glad he doesn't drag it out. He doesn't even wait for me to acknowledge it. He gets up and heads straight for Liam, who opens his arms and immediately wraps them around his boyfriend's waist. My best friend looks... in love.

I wish I could say *good for him* and mean it, but the words feel like a lie, even in the privacy of my own thoughts. There's a sense of wistfulness as I dwell on it. I wanted that with him for so long. I'm glad he's happy. I am. But I'm kind of... not. I'm not glad because I'm a piece of shit plagued by jealousy. I can't be happy for him. Not exactly. I just want what they have too badly.

Well, not what they have exactly. There's a softness about Liam when he's around Sebastian, and I can admit that I never pictured that when I imagined us together. Thinking back, I don't think I even knew what I wanted from him—other than something more than friendship.

That's not the case anymore. I'm as over him as I can expect. Now, I have no idea what I want, but I know it's not *this*—this sense of being surrounded by people but feeling alone. Plus, Nic. Being stuck in a mess of *I'm not good enough,* and *nobody wants me* is bad enough without having to deal with a case of Dumb Dick on top of it.

It's a condition. Possibly a mental disorder. It has me picturing Nic and me in the happy couple's places, and the image makes everything worse—the mellow ache of loneliness amped up. It's not believable and yet, I don't hate it. But Nic isn't that. He's not any sort of soft or nice, and even knowing that doesn't keep me from imagining it.

Liam gives his boyfriend a quick peck on the lips, and I sigh. That has the image in front of me evaporating. Nic would never do that—let *me* do that. I'm just too jealous to be happy for my best friend.

"He rejected you, and you still can't move on," the cause of said Dumb Dick says, and for a moment, I'm too confused to react. "It's no wonder. It's pretty pathetic—of course he doesn't want you. Who would?"

I open my mouth to respond, but what can I say? His words pick at the insecurities I was already wallowing in. The word *nobody* is playing on a loop in my head as an answer to his question, and it's true. Nobody wants me. Nobody I want anyway. Not Liam. Definitely not Nic.

No, he's made that abundantly clear.

Nic makes me stupid, makes it hard to conjure up any wit. So I say nothing—let him win and simply watch as he gets up and leaves the room.

Why? It's a question I ask myself a lot. There's nothing wrong with me. I know I look good. Personality-wise, well, that's subjective. But passable.

I shouldn't be giving these thoughts any attention, but it cannot be helped. Sexual frustration is hell. And worse than that was the reprieve I felt because of *him*. Getting a taste of calm just to have it stripped away far too soon.

Nic had me satiated for mere moments before he fucked it all up. Not long at all, and yet my brain and this Dumb Dick I'm stuck with have come to associate him with peace. It's laughable.

But he could do it again—give it to me again. If he just fucking would. And god, do I want that. But he. Doesn't. Want. Me.

Bullshit. It's bullshit. I feel like stomping my feet, flopping on the floor, and banging my fists. Why not? *Why?* Fucking fuckhead. I'm a goddamn catch. Sexy and... I'm hot, dammit!

I feel like I need to show him. I will. I am. Right now.

I get up and head down the hall, leaving the rest of the apartment without any goodbye so that I can do that very thing. Yup. I'll fucking show him.

Nine

Nic

I've always known about Cade's obsession with Liam. Liam, the baseball player, the happy-go-lucky jock who couldn't give a fuck less about... anything. Girls, the gym, and baseball. Baby was right. *Pretty but not the sharpest tool in the shed.*

He's not dumb. Clueless maybe. There were a lot of moments where I could see Cade's longing when they were together. He'd stare at his best friend and look so dejected, and Liam never once noticed. Not that Cade let him.

I didn't have any expectations, but I'm not surprised that nothing has changed. But how fucking hopeless could he be? The guy has a boyfriend. Move on.

And Baby was right. He's a big dude, Sebastian. Easily the tallest person in the room—even with Logan there—and looked pissed off at seemingly nothing unless Liam was looking at him. I could so see him punching Cade in the face.

Fuck, sometimes I want to punch him in the face. Watching him pathetically pine over a person who had his arms wrapped around some other guy—I wanted to hit him just to knock some sense into him. Idiot.

How does one go from saying my name while coming to pining over someone else not even twenty-four hours later?

I brush my teeth aggressively until I realize I'm being stupid. I don't know why I'm so upset anyway. Fuck him. And Liam. And Sebastian. And he didn't do much, but fuck Logan too.

Baby's the only tolerable person in the apartment at the moment.

Even I'm getting on my nerves.

I spit in the sink and the sight of dried toothpaste has me close to fuming. He is the actual worst. Uncivilized. How hard is it to rinse the sink when you're done?

I grab his face towel off the rack to clean his mess up and then try to hurry and get dressed only to hiss when the fabric drags over the top of my left leg.

Sitting on the ground stretched my muscles, leaving my thighs burning about halfway through the movie. I didn't even move to try and fix it, too worried Cade would once again mother hen the fuck out of me in front of his friends.

The scarring isn't the worst. I didn't use the same methods as a lot of people and it wasn't that long before I was found out anyway. But when they hurt, it's never one type of pain. There's a strain from the way the skin pulls, the scar tissue pulling too tight to even allow a proper stretch. There's a dull ache that goes deep, and at times, it feels like the most painful, the most unmanageable because it goes too deep for any of the topical treatments to work. That one kind of sneaks up on me at times.

But the worst of it is the burning. It makes the skin hot to the touch, and no amount of rubbing it with anything fixes it. It's shallow and makes my skin itch, but it can't be scratched because that only makes it worse. And this kind of pain does not sneak up. It demands attention. It's kind of ironic—that same sensation used to calm me, and now it only drives me crazy.

But like it did back then, it does take my mind off of other things.

I breathe through it for a few seconds as I debate going back out there to get some ice. But I don't want all of them to look at me. So I pull my sweats up the rest of the way, accepting that there's no real solution. The ice wouldn't help much either way. I just need to lie down and, hopefully, sleep through it.

Only as soon as I open the door my plans are shattered. I get a full view of Cade's bare ass as he digs around his drawer, and I'm pissed off all over again.

"Can you not?"

He doesn't even have the decency to try to cover up or look embarrassed that I caught him naked. He just stays doing what he's doing—probably dragging it out just to fuck with me. As I think about last night, it makes sense. He has no shame.

"You don't have to look."

I scoff at that. It's utter bullshit. "You do everything you can to make sure I look at you, Cade—fucking attention whore." He is. Even earlier, choosing to sit by me and move closer when he knew I'd rather he sit anywhere else. He wants me to notice him. He makes sure I'm thinking about him. This is just another one of those little displays.

He pauses when he finally pulls his briefs over his hips, covering the unblemished globes of his ass in a deep red fabric that clings to him like a second skin. Might as well have left them off. "Why do you give it to me?" he asks with his back still to me, and I force my eyes off of his ass, letting them trail up his spine to his broad shoulders.

The slick sounds of him stroking himself are still fresh in my mind. Those breathless and desperate little noises as he brought himself closer and closer, my voice pushing him there.

I shake my head. "Give you what?" I make myself ask even though I'm not sure I want to know. It's better than the silence. The heat swirling in my abs has my stomach tightening, and it's not something I want to acknowledge.

"Your attention. You can't stand to look at me, yet you do." He finally turns around, and when his gaze sweeps across my chest, I regret not grabbing a shirt.

"Why do you want me to?"

"It's a great ass." He shrugs with a cocky grin that I'd love to smack off his face. It *is* a great ass. It's just too bad it's attached to such an infuriating boy. Seems like a waste. "Someone should be looking at it."

"Why do you want *me* to look at you?" I'm being antagonistic, but I genuinely want to know. What is with this obsession with me? But based on the look he's giving me at the moment, I'm not sure even he knows.

After a fruitless moment of searching for an answer, he ends up rubbing his face with a frustrated little growl. "I'm just horny."

I... do not have a response to that—can only watch him as he crosses his arms to try and cover himself. I guess he does have some shame then. But all it does is squeeze his pecs together, and I have to force myself not to fixate on them.

I don't know how to take what he's saying. It's self-explanatory but somehow makes zero sense at the same time.

"It's not *you*. I hate you just as much as you hate me, Nic. I'm just fucking... I don't even know! You look all..." A manic-sounding laugh cuts through his train of thought. "You know how you look," he sneers like I was about to argue or something. I wasn't. I have no reply because I have no clue what to say to *that*. "Wearing your slutty pants—don't act like you don't know what you're doing."

A laugh starts to bubble out of my chest, but it's cut short when I look down to eye my sweats. Yeah. I left my boxers off, opting for comfort, and grey sweatpants don't hide much. But still. *Is he saying he likes how I look?* "You're not making sense."

"You're hot, you dumb fuck. You—" His face

flushes at the admission, but he barrels through it before I have time to react. "You don't think I am?"

My mouth falls open, brows dipping because *what* is going on? How is this up for discussion right now —knowing me, why would he put that out there? So many questions.

Of course I think he's hot. Doesn't everyone? I'm not going to stroke his little ego, though.

"What does that have to do with any of this?"

"So you do?"

"I didn't say that." And I would never. He has access to a mirror. "This is stupid. Go to fucking bed."

"No. Not til..." His face falls, still pink as his shoulders slump like he's lost the will to keep this going. I don't know for sure what he wanted or what was going through his head as he said all of that, but I can guess.

And maybe I want it too.

There are things in my life that cannot be explained, and this is for sure one of them. Cade is out of my league. He could find anyone, a girl or boy who he actually likes. Someone who treats him like a person and not competition. Someone not so mentally fucked. Someone not so physically fucked.

"What do you want from me, Cade?" I don't bother hiding the exasperation in my voice. "You want to come?" I ask, not letting him drag it out. "Don't," I warn when he opens his mouth to argue. "I've told you, I'm not rewarding bad behavior, little brother. If you want something, you need to be a big boy and ask for it."

"Fuck you."

A smile, not at all kind, splits my face. "Fuck *you*," I correct because that's what this is. It's what he wants. He's once again begging—this time for something we both want. "That's what you need, isn't it?" My lips twitch when his arms tighten, pushing his pecs together that much more. It's obscene. A bit ridiculous.

He looks beyond pissed, standing there in just his briefs as his face washes red. He's always worked out, and he has the body to prove it. His abs are something I've worked hard to have myself, but even so, they don't look like his. Perfect. Hills and valleys that taper down into a sexy V.

I can't believe he had the audacity to ask if I find him attractive. I have eyes.

It's why I get to see it as his cock starts to stiffen. I swallow, adjusting my stance so I'm not mirroring him too closely. But it's no use. My body is reacting to his, to this sexually charged air he's trying to suffocate me with.

I take a couple of steps towards him, reveling in the nervous tick his jaw gives. He's practically vibrating, putting so much need on display. It's a heady thing, all this power he's given me.

"Ask nicely." My voice slips between us huskily, has him huffing out a breath hard enough that I feel it before he throws his head back in frustration.

"God, what is wrong with you?" He slides a rough hand through his hair, giving it a sharp tug.

"Try again."

Come on, Cade, I silently beg. I hope he gives in. I know that he wants it, but it's getting harder to deny that I do too.

"Eat shit!" He shoves at me with barely enough force to move me.

Ugh. It's a shame my dick still wants him. "Yeah, I can see why Liam passed on all this." I take a step back to eye his frame disapprovingly, more for show than anything. There's a little wet spot on his briefs that I make sure to give a little extra attention to. "With you being so desperate to give it up, I had to wonder, but—"

His fist connects with my jaw, and I react on instinct. There's a struggle—not much of one—that ends with him once again facing the dresser, cheek pressed onto the surface as I hold him there, one arm behind his back.

"That wasn't very nice." I ignore the throbbing in my face and tighten my grip on him when he tries to move. The hold has him trying harder, and when he bucks beneath me, all it does is press his ass right against my groin, and then he gives up. Just like that —the feel of my stiff cock silencing him. The only sounds in the room are our breaths, heavy and ragged. "You want it so badly, Cade." I lean over his back, fight a groan as my dick slots easily against his crease. "All I need is a *please, Nic*. Say it, and it's yours."

He shivers as my mouth skims over his ear. "No. I don't—" He drags in a shaky breath and twists his head, trying to get away from me, even as he presses his ass up against me. "I'm not saying that. This has nothing to do with you. It's—we're just getting off. I could do that with anyone."

I force out a laugh as my forehead rests on his shoulder blade. He *could* do that with anyone. But he wants me, and I have to remind myself of that.

"Okay. Sure. We can pretend." If he wants to keep my name off his tongue for now, I can let that slide. It won't last long. "But I do need to hear you beg."

I don't even know why. I just want it, and if I'm giving him something, I deserve something in return. "Beg." I'm being an asshole, but fuck. It'd sound so good. I can't see his mouth, but I can picture how his lips would look as he'd do it. Swear I can hear it, feel it in my balls as I imagine it.

"I fucking hate you," he seethes. "You—*nngh*." His hips jerk as my hand slides over his needy dick, pressing into the touch as best as he can because, despite his petulance, he wants it. My touch. Me.

"Give in," I speak the command against the bend of his neck, giving him a squeeze that drags out a guttural groan.

"*Nic.*"

I don't rub it in. Just let myself enjoy the burst of self-righteousness that flares in my chest at hearing my name in this boy's mouth and run my nose down his neck, silently breathing him in. My hand tightens until he hisses and I let go completely to move it somewhere else. I have to ignore the noise of complaint he lets out before my fingers skirt over his skin, a featherlight touch over his treasure trail. It feels like I'm teasing both of us.

"Let's hear it."

He gives me a whimper, a muted little whine that sounds like a complaint more than anything. Like he's upset with himself for giving me so much. It's so much better than the plea I wanted, and my cock throbs.

"Nic, *please.*"

Ten

Cade

I regret saying it. Especially in that voice, so small and weak sounding—it didn't even sound like me. But maybe that's a good thing. I don't really feel like myself. Maybe pretending I'm someone else will make this easier.

But then his hand slips under the hem of my briefs, and I remember exactly why I said it.

When his fingers wrap around me, I can't help but say it again. *"Nic,"* I gasp, shuffling my feet to widen my stance. I moan at the perfect pressure as he drags his fist down. It's almost too tight, reminding me of who it is that's touching me because he doesn't seem like the person to ever take shit easy. It's perfect.

"Nic, I—"

He lets go, freeing the arm he had trapped behind my back—which is nice—and my dick—which is less nice.

"Get on the bed," he orders before I have time to complain, his voice dry. The lack of emotion has me wanting to look at him, maybe see what he's feeling, but I think better of it. Don't want to ruin this. He could change his mind at any time, and then I might cry out of sexual frustration. Or punch him again, I don't know.

He was lying when he said nothing about me makes his dick hard. I *felt* that shit, his cock hard against me. It's a good feeling. Validating in an I-need-therapy kind of way. But he's into it, me. At least sexually, and I can't help but enjoy that. I'm just soaking all this attention right the fuck up, and I want it—*need it*—enough to not overthink things.

Listening to him is a means to get what I want, so I do just that. I move for the bed closest to us, to his, but he uses a hand to shove me towards mine instead. I huff as I stumble, but I don't want my big mouth to pop this semi-sexy bubble we're floating in, so I say nothing as I climb over my unmade bed.

He laughs, and I look over my shoulder to see why. "What?" I snap, feeling self-conscious as he just stands there and watches me.

"Nothing. You just got right into position, ass up like a good little slut."

I grunt, unsure how to react. My shoulders tense, but I can feel every inch of my skin—nipples peaked and balls hugging the base of my dick tightly—and I sort of love it. There's a plea on the tip of my tongue, but I don't know what it is—stop, more. I just don't know.

It was instinct to get on my knees, comfortable. He wants me to be embarrassed, but I don't want to give him that—don't want him to know that I kind of like the indignity that comes with him calling me out. I walk around like I'm sure of myself, someone who knows who he is, but it's an act. Lately the only time I'm not playing that role is around Nic. I just can't seem to keep it going around him. It's relieving to give it up.

But, fuck, do I have to give it up so easily?

"Well, do you want me on my back?" I snark. There's no way. I don't want that either. Having to watch him as he...

I wouldn't survive that.

He ignores the question. "Supplies?"

I huff a quiet breath as I place my forehead on my pillow, feeling nervous as what we're doing becomes something real. Something that I want is actually happening, and my starved self is overwhelmed.

"My sock drawer." I move my hands under my pillow, hiding them away as I grip my sheet and force myself to breathe slowly.

He's silent as he finds what he needs, stays that way as he moves behind me. All I can hear are the sounds of my own breaths, my heart thundering in my ears as he touches me.

It's not rough or hard. It's not Nic, and I fight the urge to squirm as my briefs are slowly dragged over the swell of my ass. Too quiet, too gentle. It's confusing me.

I bite my lips to keep my complaints at bay, certain that they'd only piss him off. But when I feel him spread my cheeks apart and my shoulders bunch up, my body fighting a shiver, all he does is hum a quiet noise of reassurance.

This isn't what I wanted—this *softness*.

"*Hurry*." I buck my hips, trying to urge him on, but he only seems to move slower. "Nic."

"Shh." His hands squeeze a handful each, still being too gentle, and then they're gone altogether. I hear the sounds of the lube opening, and I can't stop my hips from jerking again. My underwear is still wrapped around my thighs, making it hard to spread them further, but the feel of his finger right *there* has me trying anyway. "I just have to stretch—"

"Then fucking do it!" My hips jerk again, pressing back against his hand in a fruitless attempt to get what I need.

"Be patient." He huffs when I shuffle impatiently on my knees. "I don't want to go too fast, you—"

His name tumbles out of my mouth with a frustrated laugh before I arch my back a bit. It's clear that I want this more than him. If our places were reversed, I'd already be balls deep inside him —wouldn't be able to help myself. So, fuck him for having the audacity to be so calm about this. "I swear to god, Nic. Just get inside me." I need him to hurry before he does something stupid—like change his mind.

The smack is unexpected and rings loudly in the room as my face heats at the renewed rush of indignance.

"Patience." His voice is calm and steady like he didn't just burn my asscheeck. I almost tell him to go fuck himself, but that's the exact opposite of what I want at the moment, so I close my mouth. And then a finger is slipping in easily, pulling a little whimper out of me at the slight stretch, but with all the lube it's just not enough.

"*Nic.*"

"I—you need this, Cade. I can't just slam it in." He pulls his finger almost all the way out, twisting it as it goes, and a whole lot of feel-good shit zips straight to my sac, has them going firm against the base of my heavy cock.

"I can take more."

"Have you ever bottomed?" His voice is unsure, and I know that if I tell him the truth, he'll end this whole thing before it even starts. But despite the hesitancy in his voice, that digit stays moving inside me, and it settles a piece of me. It has my errant thoughts, my self-doubt going quiet, and I fucking want that so badly. It's addictive, that little sliver of peace.

He asked me a question, but instead of answering, I moan and hope that it's enough to distract him—to keep this going. But of course it isn't.

"Cade, have you—"

I push up onto my hands to glare at him over my shoulder. "We're not making love, asshole. If I wanted this pussy shit, I'd—*ah!*" I gasp, falling to my forearms as he shoves enough inside me to actually stretch me open. I think he skipped number two and just went straight to three. "*Ow,*" I say out loud, my face burning as the taunting backfires.

"Yeah," he chuckles darkly, leaning over me so that I hear his hushed voice clearly. "That's what I thought. Behave, little slut."

I throw back an elbow, hear him grunt as it connects with his ribs. And when his hand fists in my hair and forces my head down until my chest has my arms trapped against the bed, I don't have it in me to regret the hit.

"Do you want me to stop?" He fucks me with those fingers despite the threat—no more slow and steady as he rushes through the prep—and the only response I can manage is a frustrated grunt. It's both too long and not long enough when he finally pulls his fingers out, and as much as having them in me hurts, the way my hole clenches around nothing so suddenly is worse.

All the fight fizzles right out of me when I hear a soft crinkle of foil behind me. I'm forced to listen over the pounding of my heart, the subtle ringing in my ears as he gets himself ready, more wet sounds of lube, and then he's notched right at my entrance.

"You better be fucking sure that this is what you want, Cade."

A shiver ripples through me—a little fear, a little excitement—and all I do is nod. It's going to hurt. I know it is, but the worry is far overshadowed by all the lust coursing through my body. I'm fucking burning with it.

"Tell me you want it." He tightens his grip on my scalp, and I hiss.

"Fuck off." He knows I do.

"Come on." He leans back over me, mouth right next to my ear as his voice goes smooth. "Where'd that good little slut go, huh?" The very tip of his dick pops through, and I choke on a startled gasp, this time not saying the *ow* I feel. "I mean it." His voice changes, no longer teasing. "I need a yes, or this is over." Like it's that easy for him, doesn't matter either way.

I shouldn't be here, under him and so willing. But it seems that all my self-respect has evaporated. Gone. And it's his fault.

"Just... fucking do it." I turn my face until it's pressed hard against my pillow to hide a whimper, head still trapped under his hold.

He laughs again—always fucking laughing—and it's all the warning I get before I'm being ripped apart.

My scream is silent as all the air is forced out of my lungs, my mouth open wide against the fabric of my pillowcase. It takes my mind a few moments to come to, my whole being too wrapped up in the pain of it to be aware of anything else. My ears are ringing loudly now, keeping me from hearing the start of his moaning, the sound of Nic savoring the tightness wrapped around his cock. That sound, muffled by all the blood rushing to my ears, it helps. It keeps me from panicking too much, the evidence that I'm making him feel good.

It's a struggle for him to get all the way in. It takes several shallow thrusts to fuck me open enough before he's buried inside me. And then he stays there, hips flush against my ass as he gives me time to get used to him. My breaths are ragged, stammering out of me in shallow huffs.

But it... it's okay. Good. Leaves my head empty and body full. It was brutal, and now it's calm. It's still painful, but he's inside me, and it's everything I wanted.

"Move." It's an order spoken in a voice that still doesn't feel like mine, sounds like my head is underwater as I listen to it. "Move," I try again, tongue lolling a bit. But he does it, drags his cock out in an agonizingly slow pull, and I'm a moaning mess by the time all that's left is his cockhead. I see it coming, and my hands try to tighten the grip they have on my sheet, but there's no point—I'm already white-knuckling the cotton by the time he's forcing his way back in.

My body protests when I push back against him, impaling myself once again and triggering another white-hot pang deep in my guts. But it's worth it, gets me what I want—*more.* He listens, stays moving, and starts fucking his way in and out in violent thrusts. It's not until his hand wraps around my dripping cock and tugs that I realize I'm now achingly hard after having gone soft. The pleasure of those strokes slithers around the pain, and I start to float in it.

My head feels blissfully numb as he continues to fuck me, and I can't pinpoint when the hurt morphs into something so fucking good, but I know that I'm completely lost in it.

He groans, a drawn-out noise that stutters with every thrust, and I have to push a hand flat onto the headboard so I don't move too much. I make sure I stay right where I am so this never fucking ends.

It hits me that it will end, disappear, and the very thought has a tortured whine filling the air around us, getting mixed up in the continuous masochistic pleasure assaulting my entire being. Nic eats it up—hums like he's basking in the sound of it, taking credit for it.

"*God*. You were made for this, Cade." He moans, the sound starting deep in his chest, and I can't help but match it with one of my own. "Such a good fucking toy," he speaks softly, a filthy praise pressed right into the shell of my ear, and I have to turn my head in a clumsy attempt to seek him out, try and get a taste of those words. My every muscle pulls tight, a delicious heat licking at the base of my spine every time his balls slap against mine. "You're so fucking tight, little brother."

"*Oh, god,*" I mutter, opening my bleary eyes in more ways than one to find him looking at me. How did I let something so monumental slip my mind?

His hand curls around my balls, giving them a gentle roll that doesn't quite match the way his fat cock is pushing into me. "Shh," he whispers, his chest settling over me in a way that makes me feel safe. He feels so good, smells so good pressed against me. "Don't worry about that. Your whole purpose is this—being nothing more than a tight hole for me. That's all you are right now." He sits up, making it so I can't see his face anymore, and then I try to do what he says.

I groan, overcome with all the euphoria flooding my senses. This—it's everything. Exactly what I wanted. What I needed. No worries, no stress, no feelings of worthlessness. It's why I pushed him, pushed myself past the blinding ache of those first thrusts. Just *this*. My entire existence simplified into being nothing more than his to use. A toy. A hole.

His hand works me over in time with his hips, a single stroke paired with every punch at my insides. The unbearable pleasure-pain of it all is building. It's more, more, more. *Almost...*

I cry out as my orgasm barrels through me, and all Nic does is fuck me through it, hand fisted around my dick while my cum sprays onto the mattress beneath us. When he finally stops his brutal fuck, both of us are breathing heavily, panting noisily as our bodies struggle to settle.

"That was..." It's too much effort to finish, the words too heavy. I'm not sure I know what I would say, what the end of that sentence even is. Amazing, so fucking good. Perfect.

A mistake.

That's what he probably thinks.

There's a sheen of sweat blanketing my body, making it cold now that my blood isn't pumping quite so unyieldingly, and I'm left trembling because of it. The adrenaline drop is hitting me hard. Or maybe it's the severity of what it is we just did. Either way, I don't want him to ruin what that was by being himself.

"Get off." The words are grunted, hoarse.

I'm close to freaking out, have to turn my face again so that he can't see me. I'm waiting for a punishment of sorts—like he's going to be pissed that

I got us here.

"Cade." His voice is calm, almost cautious, and it makes everything worse.

"Get off of me." I hiss as he pulls out in a hurry, not expecting the burn the emptiness triggers. He's still holding my soft, oversensitive cock in his warm palm —the touch gentle—and I move quickly to push his hand away.

"You're shaking."

"I'm fine," I say again, almost sounding like I mean it. I might not be, though. Not if he didn't come. "I —did you..." I think he was still hard when he broke the connection. It felt like I was still stretched wide around him as he pulled out, which means he didn't get anything out of it. He could have. I wanted him to, almost wanted it more than my own pleasure. It's like last night all over again, only worse.

Nothing but a hole, and not even a good one.

"Maybe you—do you need a drink? Or..."

"What?" I look over my shoulder, find myself feeling awkward at the position I'm still in. "No—"

"Cade, you wanted it." He sounds mad.

I don't argue. We went over that already. "And you didn't?" I quip back, but really, I'm not all that sure. My muscles protest as I begin to move. I have to fight the urge to stretch out as I lay on my stomach, legs splayed outward because he's still behind me. I pretend I don't feel the cooling puddle of cum in my way. Or the throbbing in my ass.

"I clearly did."

"But I wasn't—" I clear my throat, stop myself

from saying something so embarrassing. "You didn't come." That's not much better.

"You—"

"You don't want to?" I can take more. If he needs it —wants it—he can have it. But he's silent behind me for long enough that the sting of rejection pisses me off.

"I don't think—"

"Whatever." I start to sit up, the feeling of nakedness pushing me into shaky motion. I don't want to hear the bullshit insult he's got locked and loaded. This was my fuck up, and I don't need him to emphasize that. "Move." I start to push at him, my hand barely touching him before my stare gets stuck, rudely focused on his thighs—on the scarring I never had a chance to see before now.

It's not what I expected. I assumed he cut himself because what else would it have been? But those are not the kinds of scars you get from a blade. They're textured, raised high, and bumpy in some places and pulled tight and concaved in others. Sort of shiny. I see them stretch as he stiffens, but then he's moving too.

"They're burns," I muse aloud when he stands up, regretting it as he bends over and snatches his sweats off the ground. He tugs them on hurriedly, only stopping to take the empty condom off.

He was hard, but he's not now. I did that—killed his boner.

"Sorry," I murmur, meaning it. But he ignores me. He drags a hand through his hair right there in the middle of the room, sort of awkward about it as his

123

free hand grips the side of his leg, thumb digging until the nail goes white. I wonder briefly if that hurts because of all that scarring... does he feel it? What kind of damage do burns like that do?

I'll most likely never know and never bring it up again. Not if it makes him act like this. It's like he has no clue what to do now. It makes me feel like shit, which is stupid. He just wrecked my ass, the first person I ever let do it, and he didn't even have the courtesy to come.

It hits me that it's a stupid thing to be mad at, and that only makes me feel worse. More guilty. The guiltiest for some stupid fucking reason my brain doesn't want to clue me in on. This case of Dumb Dick isn't a joke anymore. I'm stupid with lust, literally. And all this post-sex haze is no better. A symptom, because why should I feel bad for *Nic?*

But he leaves the room. Turns right around and walks out without even looking at me.

I look down at the cum smeared on my abs and the world's dumbest dick and sigh.

Eleven

Cade

"**N**ic seems different."

"I guess," I grouse, but Liam ignores the tone. It's been a week since I made a fool out of myself and started ignoring Nic altogether because of it, but it's proving harder than I thought it'd be. He demands attention just by existing. And it doesn't help that we share a room and bathroom. And we work together. I get small breaks, like now—another trip to the gym with Liam—but when I go home, he's there. I moved my study sessions to the library, but no matter how much I linger, I always end up at home. And he'll just be there, laying in bed like the moody fucker he is. Eerily silent.

"He's kinda..."

I peep the small smile on Liam's face and roll my eyes. My jaw tenses with the words he lets hang in the air. He's stupid hot, that's what he's not saying. Nicolas Aldana is all sorts of sexy. But also... "He's an asshole."

Liam hums in thought. "Sure. But also—"

"I'm gonna tell your boyfriend if you finish that sentence."

Liam cocks a brow at me before shrugging. "He has eyes, dude. Bash would agree with me—Nic is model-level attractive. He could be the male version of Winnie Harlow—that model with vitiligo."

"Don't care," I snark. "Do you only like dickheads? People who are straight fucking trash, that all that does it for you?"

That's not really fair, but honestly, he's *my* friend. Liam never liked Nic when we were teens, and as my friend, it needs to stay that way. He needs to be on my side. For my sanity. Nic isn't gonna get any less hot, and I need the people in my life to stop acknowledging it before I flip the fuck out.

"Bash is not trash." He looks genuinely offended, angry at my poor choice of words.

"Sorry." I hold my palms up, not touching that topic. Sebastian seems like a good enough boyfriend, albeit hella possessive and protective. But that's... I get why Liam likes it—he seems to eat all the attention Sebastian gives him, and I don't blame him. "Nic is, though."

"You guys haven't been getting along?"

"What do you think?" I have to duck my head to hide the faint blush I feel spreading on my face.

"Are you ready to go?" Sebastian walks up and stands aloof as he intrudes. An apathetic robot ninety percent of the time. If you take Liam out of that whole equation, Sebastian is nothing more than a quiet grump who glares a lot. It's not until Liam reaches for his hand that his browline relaxes, and it's odd how much that changes his face. From a slightly scary man to... a guy letting his boyfriend kiss his face all over.

He allows it for a moment before trying to duck away, which clearly only eggs Liam on.

"Awe. My widdle baby," he coos, and my lips crack into a curious grin as this spectacle unfolds. When Sebastian actually blushes, I have to laugh.

"Stop," he grumbles, halfheartedly pushing at the hands Liam is trying to cradle his face with. Liam presses a hard kiss onto his mouth and I have to look away, feeling like I'm the one intruding all of a sudden, a subtle ache in my chest as I listen.

I want that. Someone to kiss my face, to let me do the same. They're so publicly in love, and it makes me feel like I'm missing out. It's gross.

When I don't hear any more smooches, I return my focus to them and catch it when Sebastian seems to realize that I'm still there. His face falls, settles back into his signature scowl but not in a way that tells me he's mad. A little uncomfortable, maybe. Embarrassed.

I get it. It's awkward for me too. I'm lucky that he's cool enough to try and be okay with me hanging around—especially when Liam pushes things at times. Like now, as he asks if I want to come over to his and Sebastian's place.

I decline, telling him I have studying to do, which isn't technically a lie. We have finals coming up, but I'm pretty confident in most of my classes. Avoiding the bane of my existence means that I've logged loads of studying time.

But I've hit enough books for the day, and I don't feel like going at it again in fear of brain rot. Most likely, I'm going to head home. Sit in the living room for as long as I can until I have to go to bed. Next to Nic.

"Next time, then." He smiles easily, not at all miffed at my avoidance tactic. "I'll see you tomorrow."

"Alright." I hold back a *love you* as they walk away. Things are slowly getting better between us—the *three* of us—but I don't think that's an okay thing to say to Liam anymore. Sebastian made it clear that there are boundaries I can't cross. It doesn't feel like the kind of love I was suffocating in for a few years, not after *that* rejection, but he's still the closest thing I have to a brother, and I do love him.

I huff a laugh through my nose at the thought— I once again forgot that Nic is technically my brother. I'm silently professing my brotherly love for the guy I spent years attracted to. And now here I am, all kinds of fucked up over the guy who is legally a part of my family.

The stepbrother who hates me. Doesn't want me.

But he fucked me like he does. I felt the evidence of that for days afterward, an ache to remind me of my fuck up in a way that made my groin feel hot. It's gone now, almost a week later. I kind of miss it, and that thought pisses me off. It's not even the first time I've had it.

I need to find somebody who... is not Nic. Move on to better, healthier things.

∞ ∞ ∞

"D o I know you?" I peer at his face and swear I've seen him before. But as I look him over, my mind doesn't connect the dots.

"I don't think so. I'm Corby." He grins as he holds his hand out, and I frown at it. Who shakes hands at clubs? It makes me wish I'd just gone home, because now that I'm here, at Class, it's feeling like more work than I wanted. I'm irritable and not in the mood for flirting. It's throwing the few people that have tried off.

I swear I've seen him before. It shouldn't bother me, but then I see the last person I want to walk up behind him and groan. That's where I know him from. He's the skeevy guy Nic met on our last trip here.

"What are *you* doing here?" My stomach tightens in a warm knot as Nic looks at me. There have been plenty of guys all over me since I showed up, but I dodged all of them. None of them stirred any interest. I've been chasing the feeling all night, but now that it's here, I want to scream. *Wrong fucking guy, Dumb Dick.*

I have to constantly remind myself of that. He's the wrong guy, and it needs to be that simple. He's mean. He doesn't like me. He's my stepbrother—that alone should be enough of a reason to stomp on the massive brain boner he gives me. Except it's not. And worse, I think that's part of what gives me all those real boners I've tried and failed to ignore since last week.

"I'm guessing the same thing you are." Nic shrugs coolly, looking relaxed in a way that has me narrowing my eyes. A pissed-off Nic is the usual lately. Or always. This? I don't know what the fuck this is.

We haven't talked to each other much—not since we... I straighten up, square my shoulders as I try my best to look like a guy who is not thinking about the time his stepbrother shoved his dick in him.

The same thing you are. "You're looking for a hookup?"

There was no discernable reason for me to say that, and I wish I hadn't, but the sudden turmoil at the thought of him looking for someone to mess around with forced it out of me. He's not supposed to be here, at Class. He's a loner. He should be in his bed listening to Sleep Token or some shit.

He opens his mouth, but his buddy interrupts.

"Well, I'm here."

"What?" I half-snap at Nic's friend, irritated as I look at his face.

"You're looking for a hookup, and—"

"No." Nic couples the word with a slow shake of his head, looking at me like he thinks he can tell me what to do.

Do I want to share an orgasm with a dude named Corby? Not really. But, also, *fuck you, Nic.* "Sounds good to me," I quip, reaching for Corby's arm. I make sure I shove past Nic as I step away from the bar. It doesn't feel right as I drag this guy—the wrong, wrong guy—behind me, and when Nic catches up to us and rips my hand off of his friend, I'm mostly relieved.

Until I consider the why. Why is he so against me getting busy with his buddy? Maybe he wants Corby all to himself. My eyes ping pong between the two of them, between the angry look on Nic's face to the subdued humor on Corby's and back. "I'm not doing this."

I turn around. He can have him. He isn't that good-looking anyway. I'm for sure hotter than that guy. *Corby.* Plus, he has a stupid fucking name. That is not the kind of name anyone wants to be screaming during sex. Cade, on the other hand, is great for that.

Unless you're Nic, I guess.

I make it about halfway into the crowd before I have to admit that I have no clue what I'm doing. I'm being fueled by spite and quickly losing fire. He's here, and I should leave. That's what common sense is telling me.

I went to a different club first. A club I know Nic has never been to, where I danced with a girl for a bit before I decided that's not what I wanted. She was hot, smelled really good, and fruity, but everything about her was too delicate. Apparently, I'm in the mood to be manhandled. So, I came here. And now I'm regretting it.

But I came here to come, goddammit.

I feel unhinged. I wanted to avoid Nic—can't do that if he's here. I wanted to come—despite him, I'm going to. He's everywhere, in every part of my life, and my last orgasm can't belong to him.

Have a healthy, mutual jerk-off session with someone who actually wants to touch me. That's the mission.

Except, now all I can think about is *Nic* touching me. His hands on me. Maybe not trying to kill me. The way he fucked me. Tried to be gentle about it until I wouldn't let him. The way he talked to me. How everything he did made me feel so good when, really, it shouldn't have.

I think of his scars and how I want to apologize for seeing them. It's pushed a wedge—*another* wedge—between us, and it's driving me crazy. Guilt and regret are poisoning me, making me feel sick anytime I let myself think about it.

I think about how, despite all of that, I still want more.

A hand grips my forearm, and looking down to see it confirms what I already knew. "Why are you really here?" Nic's voice is hard to hear over all the noise, but I know it's him. I'm obsessed with his voice, with the little scratch it has. I love how deep it gets in the morning, even when I'm saving face by pretending I'm still mad at him. Honestly, I'm pretty sure I'm just obsessed with him, period.

I groan, exasperation prickling at my skin as he steps closer behind me. Regret once again swarms my insides, making my chest feel tight. I was all about getting Nic inside me. I had a goal and got what I wanted, but I was not at all prepared for the after-effects. Whether I want to admit it or not, I want him.

But he doesn't feel the same.

My eyes find his hand again, still holding my arm. *Why is he doing this to me?* He's playing with me. Fucking with my head—has to be. Enjoying the mind games because he hates me that much. But I don't deserve that.

"Getting away from you," I answer honestly, but I make sure he can't hear me.

Twelve

Nic

He's staring at my fingers, watching as they stay wrapped around his arm. I'm both darker and paler than he is, my patchy hand an odd contrast next to his flawless skin. "Cade." I loosen my grip, but I hate that and end up squeezing tighter, deciding not to let him go.

He's sort of been avoiding me, and while I know it's because of how I left things after fucking him, there's a part of me that wonders if there are other reasons. He won't look at me, hardly speaks to me—not even at work. I know he wanted it, me and the things I did to him. He did, but maybe seeing my skin like that... I don't know. Maybe it grossed him out or something.

"I told you!" He whips around—getting mad as I press the issue—ripping his arm out of my hold. "I'm here for the same reason most people come here." He waves an arm out at the crowd, and it's not hard to guess what he means.

We're surrounded on all sides by some real horny motherfuckers. Most of them aren't even subtle about it, and I'm struggling to rationalize why I'm so bothered.

"Same as you, right?" He doesn't do a very good job hiding the hurt, which almost makes me want to laugh—not because this mess is funny, though. It's not. It's frustrating as hell. It doesn't make any sense.

This is why he irks the absolute fuck out of me, why I don't understand my own obsession. Cade came here to be his horny self, probably itching to move on from his last hookup—with *me*—and he's upset about me possibly wanting the same thing?

"Go back to your—" He grits his teeth, getting visibly flustered at his own anger. Such an easy book to read. "*Corby,*" he sneers, and I wonder briefly if he's been drinking or if he's genuinely this much of a drama queen. We get caught in a stare, and I see the moment he gives up. "Nic, seriously." He sighs, his shoulders slumping resignedly. "Go away."

His cheeks are flushed, a sheen of sweat covering his face. It reminds me a little of how he looked when we fucked. I'm pretty sure that was his first time bottoming. Maybe his first time having penetrative sex with a man, period, if anything Baby says can be believed. I should probably feel bad about the way I handled him. I know I hurt him. At one point, I even wanted to. And I guess, yeah, I do feel a little guilty for it.

But he literally asked for it. Begged—fucking *moaned*—for it.

Cade ate it up. Practically went mindless beneath me, and I just... I should have had enough sense to stop myself. I thought about stopping things a lot that night, but he just kept saying *more*. Egging me on until my cock was forcing him open, and it unraveled him. Had him splitting wide open in more ways than one. It turned him into a total slut for it—the pain. Me.

That's what his problem is. He just wants *more* of that and is too stubborn to ask for it.

If I wanted to be fair, I'd be the one to give in this time. He was the one who pushed the boundaries the last time—went against his own will and asked me for it like the good little toy he was meant to be. I should relent. I can do that—I *want* to do that—if it means a redo.

Only he opens his mouth and ruins it because that's who he is.

"You weren't exactly the good lay I thought you were gonna be, Nic. Just leave me alone so I can find someone who is."

The smug as fuck look on his face as he starts to turn has me reacting. I reach out and grab him like he's mine because, for a crazy second, it feels like he is. What *the fuck* is wrong with him?

He's impossible to talk to, and I expect him to fight me. Yell at me, look at me like I disgust him, *something*. But he doesn't do any of that. He lets me dig my fingers into his wrist, and that compliance…

Fuck it.

I head toward the back of the crowded room, dragging him along with me and ignoring his halfhearted complaints. When I feel his arm slipping out of my grasp, I grip him tighter and pull until he's close enough to touch me.

"How does this whole thing work?" I look over my shoulder, having to yell a bit to make sure he hears me just before we approach the entryway being guarded by two men who are clearly bouncers.

"What?" Cade asks, playing dumb. But he can't hide the want or the embarrassment when he sneaks a glance at the hallway next to us. "The—no." He shakes his head, making his hair bounce a little. He needs a haircut. This might be the longest I've ever seen it, and the last thing I need to be thinking about is how much more grip the length could give me. "I'm not going in there with *you*."

I roll my eyes, squaring my shoulders to fight off the subtle sting those words inflict. He came here, to this club, to fuck around with someone. *In there* is exactly where he was planning on ending up.

"Yeah, you are."

It's me or nobody. Those are his options because there is no fucking way I am letting him go to *detention* with someone else. I'm giving him what he wants, what we both want. The least he can do is be grateful for it.

I know enough from what Baby and Corby have told me, so I don't wait for Cade's rebuttal before I grab him once again and pull him with me down the dark hall. It gets quieter, the thrumming of the crowd and music muffled as we round a corner, and there's another open entrance with a barely visible red glow that I'm certain is our destination. Technically, this area isn't allowed. They say it's a room to be used for peace and quiet, but in reality, it's where you go for quick hookups. Oftentimes anonymous.

A small part of me wishes this were anonymous— that he was some stranger that I could come on or in and then never see again. But mostly, I'm okay with this. I'm putting myself in this position because I crave it.

I don't crave *Cade*. It's the control he gives me. There's just something about it, something foreign and immensely satisfying about having that kind of power over someone. There's so much else in my life —everything, really—that I have no control over. So, yeah. I crave it.

But he's Cadence Howard. I've spent a lot of time hating him. He's one of the most annoying people I know. He is so entitled and full of himself, and... it's not him that I want. It's like he said. This has nothing to do with who we are and everything to do with getting off.

"I came here because I wanted literally anybody but you. I'm not going—"

"You're so full of shit." We're whispering, being quiet because that's the vibe back here. My heart is pounding louder than our voices, going rampant as he keeps being himself and fights it.

A few people slip in and out of the room before us as we stand off to the side, but we ignore them. I'm not sure why I'm even letting him argue. I can admit that the things he says bug me—that he likes to pretend he doesn't want me because the alternative is embarrassing to him—but I know him pretty well.

He's too open with me—thinks he's hiding behind an attitude that really only ends up showing me everything most of the time.

I let his arm go before turning and walking in. He'll follow me, I know it. And if he doesn't, I'll get over it.

Maybe.

It will be harder than I want it to be, that's for sure. I hate even thinking about it and have to look to make sure he is still behind me—except he's not there. And now I'm the one embarrassed. I got a little too cocky. Sort of look—and feel—stupid for it now. I stopped taking the very thing holding my mental dam together for him. I suffered through a week of shitty withdrawal symptoms—massive headaches and nausea, and for what? I told myself that he wasn't the reason, that I just wanted to come. But I wanted to come *for him.* I needed it, and now he's left me hanging.

I want to go back out there into the hallway and grab him. Take him and drag him in here. But I don't do that. He feels like mine, but that doesn't mean that he is.

My heart starts to pound harder, and I make myself stay still because I have no clue what I would do with him in front of me right now. I'm so angry, and it makes no sense. This really isn't the place for all of this, either. I can't see anything but the red glow of the LED lights and silhouettes of horny guys, hear the faint noises of people getting off, and the quiet music playing over speakers being slowly drowned out by my heartbeat the louder and louder it gets. I can smell the sex in the air. I shouldn't be in here. My eyes slip closed as I tighten my fists. They start to feel numb, and I try to focus on staying calm no matter how much worse it all gets. I need to go to my car, but my muscles are rigid, and moving doesn't feel like a good idea.

But then my eyes are open, and he's there. It's infuriating how much of a relief that is. I can't see the details of his face, can't see whatever posh outfit he's wearing tonight, but I know it's him. He steps towards me, and my stupid heart starts to slow. It goes from wild and erratic, something that makes my skin vibrate, to something that soothes me instantly when it's clear he's back in this.

I'm making all the wrong choices where he's concerned. Looking for him when I should be avoiding him. Trading shifts with coworkers so we work together, even if it's only an hour or two. Staying at home, in our room all the time, hoping he'll return like an idiot. Stopping the meds I probably still need just so I can come without knowing for sure if he even wants that from me anymore.

I am wrecking myself, and what's worse is that I'm aware I'm doing it and can't fucking stop.

I blow out a breath as he moves closer, and I can't think of a reply when he says something snarky under his breath. I'm too relieved to match his attitude as he's moving us, walking me to a corner, and I let him. Do it happily even. It almost feels like I popped a Xanax as I trail behind him. Like my body is being flooded with a flurry of euphoria instead of all of that oh-so-dramatic panic and disappointment from before.

We're always trading places. I take a step on the ladder only for him to take two, and it keeps on going that way. It's an endless cycle where neither of us is ever winning for very long. I dragged him here, yet he's in control now. Literally walking me like a dog to an empty spot amidst all the hedonism in the room.

The realization instantly pisses me off in a way that only Cade can manage. I trade places with him until his back hits the wall with a muted thud, and he's facing me. He doesn't fight me at all. It takes so little effort that it has my cock stirring.

I love this compliance—something I rarely see from him. From Cade, the stepbrother who has looked at me with contempt since the day I met him. His willingness to cede to my every whim in these moments turns me the fuck on. It's a heady thing. Undeserving in a way.

But that drugged feeling continues swirling, has everything awful inside me slipping away, making me feel almost weightless. It feels better than anything I've ever been prescribed. My heart is beating slower, and the air I'm breathing is thicker, but it's cozy and nice, and I fucking *need* it.

I'm not all that delicate with it as I push at his shoulder, forcing him to his knees. He lets out a quiet, frustrated-sounding grunt as he grabs at my hips to steady himself before I can feel him simply waiting— looking up at me in the dark as I undo my jeans on autopilot. And then it's like he can't wait anymore. It has bone-deep contentment settling into me, the way he fumbles eagerly with my briefs, taking the time to tuck the hemline under my balls.

I fight a chill as he wraps his sweaty palm around me, ready for whatever he's willing to give me in this moment. He takes me into his mouth, his velvety tongue flattening along the underside of my dick as he sinks his lips almost down to the base, and I have to place a palm on the wall above him just so I don't keel over. Of course he's good at sucking cock—he's good at fucking everything, better than me at every little thing he does.

Only this time, as I hit the opening of his throat, I can't find it in me to be all that upset about it. I let my head fall forward with a soft groan as my fingers slide through his hair—pure bliss and warmth spreading throughout my groin.

I wish I could see him, watch as Cade's mouth is stretched wide around me, his eyes watering and spit dripping down his chin as he takes every inch I give him greedily. He's quietly moaning for it, trying to swallow me down, and I'd give anything to see his face right now.

Fuck. He runs his tongue over the tip, coaxing out more precum before his lips push at my foreskin, sliding it back until he can suck on the fully exposed glans. He's tasting and savoring, so fucking hungry for it that I have to bite my lip to keep from moaning out loud. He pulls off with a slurp only to mouth at my balls while he strokes me, giving us both the chance to breathe. It's good, but not what I want, and my resolve doesn't last very long before I'm taking myself in hand so I can feed him my cock once again. My hips rock as I fuck myself deeper into his mouth, and it feels so good that I do it again. Then again.

God, I go mindless with it, the feel of his skilled mouth wrapped around me driving me almost mad. And he takes it all so well—happy to be used by me. So fucking good at it that it makes me think of all the times he's done this before, maybe even right here in this very room. I force my eyes shut, actively trying not to feed that train of thought anymore. But it can't be helped. I wonder how many guys Cade has been in this very position with, and I know I have no right to be jealous—I don't even understand why I am. But as deeply as he can take me, I feel like the number must be high. He's every bit the slut he likes to prove himself as, and it's equal parts sexy and infuriating.

His hand covering mine where it's tightened too much in his hair has me opening my eyes again, and suddenly, I'm peering down at his darkened silhouette —wishing again that I could see him clearly. I feel his eyes on me and think about easing up on him, but then I decide that's stupid. I don't know that this will ever happen again, that I'll ever get it exactly how I want it, so I'm definitely taking full advantage of it now. I move my hand from beneath his so I can cup his skull, pulling him against me as I sink in once again. I move slowly, make sure he has time to stop me and can't help but grin when he doesn't. He continues letting me use him to my liking and sits there patiently as I work my cock deep into his mouth, and it's only then, when my lips part to offer a filthy praise, that I remember everyone else in the room.

His hands grab at my ass, pulling me into him so roughly that I grunt in surprise. I can feel teeth almost at my base, his nose in my pubes, and the slick tunnel of his throat starting to panic around me as I cut off his breathing. And Cade, the boy I like to call my little brother, he fucking loves it. Choking himself on my dick brings out a moan from deep inside his chest, earning us some aggressive *shhs* from somewhere in the room.

My orgasm takes me by surprise, pulse after pulse climbing up my length with every rope of cum being spilled down his throat. I'm vaguely aware of his hands grabbing at my jeans, suffocation finally getting to be too much for him, but I'm too busy experiencing raw ecstasy to do anything but hold him in place. My very own little cock slut, so filthy and perfect.

"*Fuck*," I mutter when I finally step back, listening to Cade noisily drag in a deep breath and fight a cough. My eyes are mostly adjusted to the dim lighting, but I can still hardly see him in the red glow. I almost feel bad, watching his solid frame kneeling on the ground as he struggles to drag in oxygen.

I reach for him, help him stand, and stay close as he wobbles. My hand covers his bulge, thinking it only fair to return the favor, but there's no need. He's wet. Soaked. He came in his jeans while he was choking on me.

I'm cozy and warm with all sorts of post-nut

euphoria. And maybe a little bit of that shitty clarity one can expect after things like this. I just fucked Cadence Howard's face. My limp, tired dick is still wet with his saliva as it hangs there shamefully.

I tuck myself away as I take a step back. "We're not doing this again," I say, making sure to speak clearly so he—and who knows how many others—can hear me. And then I turn around and leave him there.

Thirteen

Cade

"I wouldn't bother."

I don't remember this guy's name, but I recognize him as Sebastian's annoying friend from when they came to the diner to rub Sebastian's first date with Liam in my face. I've only been to Liam's new place twice, and both times, I was quick to leave. I helped him move in and made sure to do nothing more than set shit down and bounce. I'm not all that sure why I even bothered coming here today.

"They're probably fucking," he continues. "They don't answer the door when that's going on. Nothing more important than Liam's ass." He doesn't even look at me as he speaks—just stares down between his knees as he sits in front of my best friend's door on their doormat. "Horny bastards," he mutters.

"That's—" but I don't know what to say to that. I still can't believe Liam is a bottom. How does one go from straight jock to... dating a guy who can kick my ass? "How long have you been here?" I don't actually care, but it feels awkward, so I'm pressured to say something that has nothing to do with Liam being fucked.

"Who knows? I used to have a key, but they have so much sex it got taken away."

"Right." I nod. "That makes sense." Not really, but it's none of my business either way.

"Did Liam know you were coming?" He looks up at me finally, hope softening his features.

I sigh. "Nope." I was antsy. Needed to do something other than obsess over Nic and figured coming here was the answer. It's really just my luck that Liam is busy.

"Well, why are you here?" he has the audacity to ask.

"Because I can be." My best friend lives here. I almost ask him why he's here, but I guess his best friend lives here too.

He rolls his eyes. "Forgot what a joy you are." He goes back to looking at the ground, and I simply don't care enough to keep the conversation going. I turn to leave, but his voice stops me. "Wait! Where are you going?"

I ignore him, go back to what I was doing, and try to think of somewhere else I can go. Can't go home. Nic isn't there, and all I'll be doing is wondering where the fuck he is. If he's avoiding me again. Maybe with someone else stupid enough to pine over him. Like fucking Corby.

"Wait," Sebastian's buddy says again, but I don't need to play nice with my friend's boyfriend's friends.

That's not a thing, or at least I don't want it to be. It's bad enough I have to be nice to the guy who broke my nose. Whoever this guy is can fuck right off. "You're Cade, right?"

I stop walking to gawk at him, wondering why he's suddenly standing next to me. "What are you doing?"

"I don't know." He shrugs a slim shoulder at me, definitely trying to irritate me if the slight curve of his lips is any indication. "Following you."

"No, you're not." Who the fuck does this guy think he is?

He snorts, tucking a few strands of dirty blonde hair behind his ears and revealing a fresh, jagged cut at his hairline. "Well, clearly I am."

I do my best to ignore the ugly bruise surrounding a smudge of crusty blood, but I know he's aware I saw it because he moves his hair over it once more. I want to ask what caused it, but I don't know him well enough to ask. But I want to know. For some reason, it reminds me of Nic. His legs and the scars he hates that I saw. I wish I hadn't looked at them, been so shocked to see the mess he made of his own legs. I wish I'd found out he was doing that to himself sooner, that I'd cared enough to pay attention so I could get him help sooner. I kind of wish I knew just how the hell he did it. Mostly, I wish—

"Where are we going?"

I scoff, try to think of an answer, and then scoff again. I want to stop thinking of Nic. He makes me feel actually crazy—the kind of nuts that makes me enjoy using cock as a cork for my throat. I can feel all the neurons in my worthless brain going feral when I think about him, and I absolutely blame that—blame Nic—for why I cave to this sort of stranger so easily.

"I have no clue."

∞∞∞

J ax can fucking talk. His ramblings have been the only thing keeping me occupied the past hour, so I'm almost grateful for it, but... holy hell, can he yap.

"Shut up." I roll my eyes. "You're so full of shit."

"Swear to god." He holds his palms up, but again, I call bullshit.

"That means nothing coming from an atheist."

Which I only know he is because he told me. I might know too much about this guy, really. He's a certified yapper and went on about it for close to fifteen minutes before he saw a quail on the sidewalk and segued into a monologue about how they mate for life.

"Okay, well... yeah. I can see that. But I'm not lying! They have like a whole dresser full of dil—"

I veer the car right, turning onto a busy road and cussing when Jax lets his nachos slide off his lap. And then cuss again when someone honks at me.

"What the fuck is your prob—"

"*Shh!*" There is zero chance that Nic can hear us, not from way up the road. But still. I don't need to listen to Jax's barking as I carry out this somewhat idiotic and very impulsive adventure right now.

"I am not cleaning that up."

"Yes, you are. And be quiet."

"Your car is gonna smell like cheese."

"Stop. Talking."

He goes silent for maybe two seconds before he brings up ants, and I groan. I decide it's best to give up, letting him spill every single thought that runs through his mind. But I barely hear any of it as I continue following the black car I saw. It's a little hard to try and make sure I stay far enough behind that Nic doesn't see me but close enough that I don't lose him.

I'm glad that Jax is too busy filling the silence to notice what I'm doing. This shit is embarrassing.

I should stop. I could take this next left right here and stop following him. I should definitely do that.

Ope, too late. Not that left, then. The next one.

But... where is he going? Not the diner, clearly. It's minutes of being a creepy stalker before I follow him onto a residential street, and then I have to drive much slower.

"Cade?"

"Huh?"

"What are we doing?"

"Nothing." I sit up straight, adjusting so I look more normal and not like I'm trying to hide behind my dash. "Why are you here again?"

"You're going ten under the speed limit. They can

actually pull you over for that. For going too slow. They might want to do a wellness check on you—my grandma was pulled over for that once. She was super high on pills, though, so I was pretty grateful." He pauses to snort. "My mom had to come to the police station and pick me up, but she was high too, so I ended up going to this Puerto Rican woman's house for a bit. Lotta people there, and I had to sleep on the floor, but the food was so fucking good. I have dreams about that lady's dinners to this day. Whose house is this?"

"Jax."

"What?"

"You talk a lot." That's really all I can think to say to all of that. Also, I have no fucking clue whose house this is. Or whose house Nic just walked into. Maybe it's Corby's. I don't know that he has any other friends.

"Yeah. I get that a lot. But why are we here?"

"I genuinely have no clue why you're here," I whisper, giving in to the urge to sink low in my seat. Just in case Nic looks out the window or something. Not that it would do any good. He knows my car. I should not have done this.

He huffs. "Whatever. I'm growing on you. I can tell."

"Sure. Like a wart."

"Whatever."

"You already said that."

"Who are we stalking?"

"What?" I sit back up, try and fail to look like someone who isn't indeed a stalker.

BRIANNA FLORES

"That car," he says, pointing with his bony finger at Nic's sedan. "We've been following it for a while."

Oh. He's more attentive than I gave him credit for. "No, we haven't," I lie.

"Now, who's full of shit?" He reaches down to the floorboard and grabs a chip. I have to stop him when he goes to put it in his mouth, shaking my head at him until he drops it again. "Just seems like a waste of perfectly good nachos."

"We'll get more," I tell him. "And I'm not following anybody. I don't know who—*down!*" I duck, and when all Jax does is look around, I have to yank on the collar of his shirt to pull him down with me, ignoring his complaints. "*Fuck.* Do you think he saw us?"

"Who?"

"He's going to be so pissed if he saw me." I know he is.

"Which one is he?"

"What do you mean? How many are there? Who else—" I sit up, just enough to peek out of my window, can't help but do it because I want—*need*—to know who he's with, but I sink back down immediately. "*Shit!*" I hiss. "He saw us. Don't be weird—"

"Dude, you're being weird."

I shut my mouth when Jax, still leaning over his knees, looks up behind me and waves.

"I get why we were stalking him."

I sit up again. Try for nonchalance as I stare at the street in front of me rather than look over at where Nic is beside my door. "I don't know what to do," I admit. "Maybe I should—we're just going to leave." I nod my head slowly, lips in a tight line as I wonder when I got so... like this.

"I don't think that's the right move, buddy. He looks pretty mad."

But if anything, that just makes me want to leave even more. I'm not sure what he'd do right now if I spoke to him. Tell him that I happened to see him and followed him because, I don't know, I just wanted to say hey?

The last time I talked to him, I ended up on my knees. Came in my jeans just at the taste of his cock. I've got a case of Dumb Dick, but Nicolas does not. His dick is... not dumb. Uncut. Fat and long. Big enough to actually cut off my air supply. I couldn't even breathe through my nose with the way he was fucking my throat. And then he ruined it.

We're not doing this again.

Yeah, fuck him. I can't face him right now. More importantly, I don't want to. His knuckles rap against my window, but I've made up my mind.

I drive off, eyes ahead so I don't look at his face.

$\infty\infty\infty$

"What the heck?" Liam stands there, blocking the entrance until Jax shoves his way past him. "Did you guys come here together?" He looks genuinely befuddled at the very possibility. I get it. I doubt there are many who willingly hang out with Jax. I find it hard to believe that Sebastian can tolerate him for very long.

"Sort of." I shrug, not feeling up to explaining the story of how it is I ended up hanging out with Jax. He'll probably explain it all himself anyway. "You gonna let me in?"

Liam steps aside just as my phone buzzes in my back pocket, and I ignore it. Again. I know it's Nic. He's been calling and texting me ever since he saw me. But I'm settled on ignoring it. Ignoring him. Procrastinating, I suppose. I know I'll have to deal with it eventually, but that's future Cade's problem. Currently, all I'm going to do is spend an awkward hour or two hanging out with Liam and his buff boyfriend.

Their dog starts immediately trying to climb up my leg, yapping in a way that reminds me of Jax when I step over the threshold. So, Liam, his buff boyfriend, and the two yappers. I've never been a super big fan of dogs. Liam loves them. Used to talk about wanting one all the time when we were younger. Liam being a dog person and finding himself a boyfriend who is the kind of guy to bring stray dogs home makes sense. No wonder I never had a chance.

In a way, it makes me feel better about the whole thing. The unrequited-ness of it all. I'm not right for Liam, never was, but maybe he's not right for me either.

"Okay. Down, girl." I try to gently push her away with my foot, but she just goes back to trying to climb up my leg. "Liam. Please control your dog."

"Rude." But he picks her up, immediately cuddling her up against his chest and cooing at her as he tries to dodge her yucky dog tongue. "So, what are you up to?" he finally asks, leaving the dog-sized rodent to squirm aimlessly in his arm.

"I'm... here." I shrug.

"Okay." He smiles. "What brings you here?"

It's Jax who answers for me, who doesn't shut up when he catches my glare. "We were stalking his boyfriend, but we got caught."

"His boyfriend?" Liam raises his eyebrows at me, mouth hiding in his mutt's fur.

"No. Not my boyfriend."

"Okay." He's enjoying this a tad too much, more excited about the prospect of me dating than even I would be. "Then who?" Liam asks, but again, Jax doesn't give me a chance to answer.

"Well, if he wasn't your boyfriend, can he be my boyfriend? He's hot as hell. Like... I can't actually think of anyone hot to compare him to, but he's gorgeous. It's his skin thing, the vital something— whatever it's called—he's almost ethereally hot."

I look up at the ceiling and wait for Liam to get it.

"Wait. Vitiligo?"

I can hear the shocked smile in his voice. Kinda want to slap it off his stupid, pretty face. Jax, just confirming what Liam already knows, has the bastard cheesing.

"Huh. That reminds me of someone. But I mean, it couldn't be. Cade hates *that* guy."

"I don't think vitiligo is that common. Like, I can think of one person I've seen with it in my life—and it's Cade's hottie. He is really... maybe I'll start stalking him."

Liam laughs, and I can feel my jaw tighten, the sound of his dumb chuckle making me irrationally angry that my supposed friend can find my misery so amusing.

"He's not—I wasn't stalking him!" I glare at Jax, but that's not wholly fair. I expected him to blab. Should have left him at the gas station like I wanted to. "I just—I wanted to see what he was doing. I was curious." I shrug. Kind of. I don't really know what all that movement was, but it doesn't do a good job of convincing either of them that I'm not a freak all sorts of hung up on his stepbrother.

Stepbrother! Fuck.

My eyes move to Liam, silently trying to beg him not to tell Jax that detail. Sometimes, I forget that even is a detail. The plot of my life is now a cheesy porno. Only with more drama than someone who wants to bust a nut would be willing to sit through.

Fourteen

Nic

"Where the fuck have you been?" I cut Baby off the literal split second Cade walks through the front door. Cade at least has the decency to blush, look a touch embarrassed at whatever the hell it was he was doing following me to Corby's earlier. And then leaving with some random guy without even talking to me. "Where have you been?" I try again in a tone that has his blush disappearing, a sneer taking its place.

"I was at Liam's. Not that it's any of your business."

It's instant, the need to correct him. "Right. And me being at my friend's house, that's *your* business?"

"What friend?" He looks appalled that I might have one, that I would be at anyone else's place.

It genuinely baffles me how someone can show all their cards like that at all times. There are no instances when I don't have a pretty good idea of what he's feeling. He has the emotional maturity of a three-year-old. This? This obsessive jealousy, like he has any fucking right, really just points out how full of himself he is. Like he has any sort of claim on me.

He doesn't. I can't deny that he feels like mine at times, but I am not and will never be something he can own. I'm not even something he wants, not really. I wouldn't give myself to someone as careless as him. I'm not that stupid. And as far as my jealousy goes, at least I hide it. I'm not humiliating myself by...

I scoff, getting flustered at my own reasoning. It feels like I'm lying to myself. I'm just as bad as him. Maybe even worse.

"Why were you following me?" I'm not giving him an answer to his question. He doesn't need to know things like that. Things about me. Cade is the last person I can see myself opening up to—about anything.

"I'm not doing this." He stalks off down the hall, and a few seconds later, I can hear our door being slammed. That's what he says when he can't think of anything to say to explain his shitty logic away.

I don't want to follow him, but as soon as I can't see him anymore, my knee starts bouncing because fuck, I want to follow him. I want to demand he tell me what he thought he was doing earlier. Why he disappeared like that. Who he was with, and if he left without talking to me because he was embarrassed by me.

That's—I get it if he was. Between the scars, the vitiligo, the general vibe of me—empty at the best times and sad and angry and broken at the worst. I get being ashamed of wanting that. I do. But why even go after me in the first place?

"You should..." Baby's hand lands on my knee, willing it to stop shaking and not continuing until it does just that. "Cade is a lot. We all know that. He likes to... argue. And complain. So, I can understand it if you don't follow him, but I mean, it's your room too." He shrugs, pulling his slim hand off my leg to turn his attention back to the TV. "And I think he wants you to. Follow him, I mean. But maybe be quieter this time? I want to go to bed soon."

"You—" I relax in my seat, taking a breath when my muscles ease. He heard us then, heard Cade being fucked. By me. I don't know why that settles me so much, but it's oddly relieving to have it acknowledged like this. That someone knows that Cade wants those things.

Someone else can see that he's mine, even if Cade can't.

And he's right. It is my room.

∞∞∞

He's in the shower, forcing me to wait for him. It feels very telling that I am actually waiting for him. Like a dog. Shit's embarrassing. Sitting here motionless while he goes on like usual. I try to reason with it by telling myself that all I'd be doing is this anyway.

It's late, I have work in the morning, and my life is otherwise boring. This is what I do most of the time: sit here looking at Cade's bed.

That's where I took him, slammed into his ass until he was nearly crying beneath me. And I didn't even get to come.

My eyes trail to my sock drawer, where my meds are. I shouldn't have quit them like that. The Zoloft mainly. It makes it impossible to finish, but then the lack of arousal makes that a nonissue anyway.

Until I moved in with Cade, and suddenly it was an issue. A big problem. It's not right being my age and not able to hit a climax. Not normal. And I'm okay, mentally. I think. I *feel* okay. Not any more anxious or sad than I already was. Maybe the pills weren't even working. If I'm going to feel all those things anyway, I might as well be able to shoot a load into my stepbrother's guts.

I lay down and roll over to stare at the wall to try and convince myself that I'm not getting turned on at the sight of his messy bed. But a second later I have to adjust myself, pull at my boxers where they've tightened. It's his fault. Nobody could live through that experience and not get all hot thinking about it.

I want a redo. It's sort of why I went cold turkey on my meds—a need to empty my balls in his hole, leave him leaking. It's made me reckless, it seems. My old therapist would be very disappointed in me.

We're not doing this again. I said that to him. For reals. What a joke.

I used to question what it is about Cade that

has people so willing to accept him, like him. It's always been hard for me to see past the bullshit. The smug aura surrounding him, the... I'm not a hundred percent sure what it is about Cadence Howard. He just aggravates me.

Now look at me. Obsessing over thoughts of him wrapped around my dick. But it cannot be helped. Hating my stepbrother makes me feel alive.

The bathroom door opening has me sitting up to face him immediately, my impatience worn too thin as is.

"Who was that guy in your car?"

I can feel a subtle throbbing in my temple, regret for the question and the way I asked it making it hard to sit still. I sound like him—childish and incapable of handling my emotions.

"Why do you care?" He's less flustered after his shower—he had some time to calm down, whereas I've done the opposite.

He makes me want to pull my hair out. Yank it right off my scalp. Guarantee I'd enjoy that feeling a lot more than *this*. Even better, I could pull on his hair. If I wasn't so sure he'd love it, I just might.

"I just want to know who was following me, Cade. And why. I don't go around chasing you like a lost puppy, do I?"

"Isn't that what you were doing last night?" he snarks. He's always gotta fight. Dealing with him is never easy—he makes sure of that. "I walked away from you then, and *you* were the one who followed—*chased*—me, Nic."

That's... he's got me there. But I think I won that round. He's the one who ended up on his knees, and when I cock a self-assured brow at him, I know he's realized the same thing. I don't want to give him time to reflect. "Just tell me."

"I—no."

"No?"

"That's what I said.." He drags his towel over his head, leaving me to stare at his mostly naked form. His briefs are black, form-fitting but dark enough that I can't see much of anything. Not behind those anyway. I can definitely see the rest of him—which I guarantee is what his conceited ass wants.

"Cade..." I have to force myself to take a breath, to calm down. It's ridiculous that such a small thing has me so worked up. Maybe I should be on a pill for *that*.

"I don't get why it's a big deal. You don't care what I'm doing or who I'm doing it with any other time."

He's wrong. I think about those very things pretty much anytime he's not around. I shouldn't. The smart thing to do would be to drop it. I harp about the way Cade can't hide any of his thoughts all the time, but I'm awfully close to behaving the exact same way on a regular basis.

"Yeah," I say, my stomach tightening in discomfort as I settle on making the right choice. "You're right—I don't care." I lay down again, and go back to looking at the wall. I can feel him behind me, still standing in the same spot. Still shirtless with his nipples peaked. Hair a little damp and dripping on shoulders. I can picture it all so well, just lying here with my eyes screwed shut. An image engrained behind my eyelids, right there next to all the other ones I have stored away of him. At this current moment, it feels like I'll never be rid of them. Of Cade.

I need to figure this life shit out. Move. Go back to pretending Cade doesn't exist. I've done fairly well letting go of most of the hate and disgust I had for his mom and my dad, but I'll never forgive them for the shit they pulled. For breaking my mom and forcing a brother who I didn't want on me.

"It was—his name is Jax. We're not, like, friends or anything. He was at Liam's when I went. I barely know him."

I let the silence following his words fill the space between us for a moment. It's a relief. I don't know if it's because he actually told me, and now I know, or if it's his compliance that has me feeling so much better all of a sudden.

"Whose house was that?"

I ignore that, smiling at the way he huffs when he realizes I'm not telling him. "Why were you following me?" I stay where I am, unmoving as I ask him again. As awful as picturing him is—his pecs and six pack, that thin happy trail, all of it—seeing it is worse.

"I... have no fucking clue." He sighs loudly, drawing it out dramatically as he flops on his mattress. "I genuinely do not know."

I mostly believe him. He can be impulsive. That's not anything new, but he has to have some idea. But the tension in the room has noticeably eased, and the last thing I want to do is crank it back up by pressing the small shit. "Well, why didn't you say hi or something?"

"Why didn't I—Nic." He huffs an exasperated laugh, prompting me to finally face him. "You get irrationally angry at pretty much anything I do. I chose life."

"It's not irrational to be pissed that you followed me to my friend's house with some fucking guy I don't know." I mimic him and fall onto my back so I don't have to look at him when familiar feelings start to bubble up again.

"You sound jealous."

I scoff, but I don't know what to say to negate that fact. It's not something I can believably deny, and saying less is probably the safest option.

"Wait. Are you?"

"You're delusional."

"Holy shit." He sounds awed, so pleased with himself that I have to flip him off. He laughs, and I'm too tired to deal with him. But when I face the wall again, he stops. "You don't—Jax is nobody. I barely tolerate him. He's more annoying than you. Well, maybe not *more* annoying, but... you don't have to be jealous of Jax."

It's tough being around Cade. So many contradictions, so much confusion. I hate that he's trying to reassure me, and I hate even more that it's working. I should have said no when Anton suggested this little setup. Me moving here, I knew it was a bad idea—a horrible, life-altering idea, and here I am anyway.

But in a weird way, even knowing all of the things I do now, I'm kind of glad that I said yes.

"Nic?"

His voice sounds different. Almost like when I had him pinned against his dresser. It has me turning around so that I can see the face paired with such a quiet and soft sound.

"Whose house was that?" He's picking at his fingers, refusing to look at me.

I watch in real-time as the insecurity grows, seeps onto his face. My chest tightens along with my hands that kind of want to reach for him. I'm more willing to share now that he's told me what I wanted to know first. "I was at Corby's." If he'd paid attention and looked instead of hiding like the world's worst spy, he would have seen Corby walk out with me. I expect the news to make him feel better, but if anything, I think it's only made things worse.

I knew he was jealous. Maybe hoped is a better word for it, but I didn't think it was of Corby specifically. He's just a friend. In the same way that Jax is Cade's friend. Corby is the kind of guy who leaves a vague sense of dislike simmering under your skin when he's around, but all in all, he's okay. Not at all someone I want to fuck, though.

"Oh."

I know that he wants me to tell him why I was there—tell him that we're just friends, but I can't do that. I won't give him that. That would put us on the same level, and that's not a good idea. Not safe.

I can give him something we both want, though.

"On your knees, little brother."

Fifteen

Nic

"I'm in here!"

"Yeah, well, I've been in your ass, so it's a little too late for modesty, Cadence." I have to look away when he pokes his shampoo-topped head out from behind the shower curtain so he doesn't see me smile.

He looks so... cute? It feels weird, but I think, yeah. Cade is fucking cute. All soaped up and glaring at me. I don't know that I've ever felt that about him—about anyone—and I don't know how to process it.

It's gross. But luckily, it only happens sometimes. Mostly, I look at him and either want to fuck him or... slap him. Not even having regular access to his ass has gotten rid of that disdain. It's lessened it, for sure—at least sometimes—but it's still there.

"Why are you even up so early? You don't work today."

"I have a final this morning." He swipes at his brow as some suds try to slide into his eye. "Get out."

"No." I actually do have to work today. I've learned to shower at night since he never grew out of his habit of hogging the bathroom in the morning, so all I need to do is wash my face and brush my teeth. Maybe shave. My facial hair comes in white at my jawline and makes my vitiligo more noticeable. Getting rid of it doesn't exactly hide it, but it's better than giving people one more thing to notice. The comments get tiring.

"I don't bother you when you're showering."

"That's because I lock the door."

"Nic—"

"Aren't you supposed to be rinsing?"

He slides the shower curtain closed, grumbling about something that gets lost in all the noise.

A fully nude Cade being so close to me does make it hard to focus on the task at hand, but I manage—only occasionally side-eyeing the curtain and wishing it was transparent. Or maybe that I was in there with him.

Or, no. Not that. I'm not sure he's seen me fully naked, not since the last time. I don't know if that's a subconscious choice on my part or a very conscious choice of his, but he has not seen my scars since then. We've had sex a handful of times. He's even taken me down his throat a few more times, but when that happens, my pants stay on.

We don't even look at each other. It's either dark, or his back is to me. Never face to face. He makes sure of it every single time.

So, that answers that—he's the one who doesn't

want to see me. And having a view of myself in the mirror kind of helps me understand the why. It's not that I look bad. I've spent time on my body and do what I can to care for it. I grew up skinny and gauntly looking, and compared to then, I know I look good. And a lot of people like my skin. They go out of their way to tell me.

But a lot of people don't. I hear that far less, but they will stare at me. They ask me what *it* is. I get how it can be off-putting, I do, but it's always a bummer to have to answer the same damn questions over and over.

Cade confuses me. There's a steady stream of contradictions where he's concerned. I feel how badly he wants me, but he doesn't want to look at me—how fucked is that?

His phone rings, his mom's face taking over the screen where it's resting by the sink.

"It's your mom." My voice is flat, my insecurities making me moodier than I was when I woke up. Plus, *her*. I can't imagine how she'd react to finding out her precious son was being defiled on the regular by *me*. Or how Anton would take it. The fuck-up corrupting the golden child would not at all go over well.

Cade gets out pretty quickly, not even bothering to dry off, as he steps towards his phone. In a split second, I can see how it'll play out. He'll answer it and walk away, talk where I can't hear him, or more importantly, so that she can't hear me.

Something in me snaps, and I'm answering his phone for him before he can get his hand on it.

"*Nic!*" he hisses, but I put it on speaker, and his mom's voice makes him go quiet just like that.

"Cade?"

He tries to take it out of my hand again, but keeping it out of reach isn't difficult, not when he's trying not to let his mommy know I'm right here. Like she doesn't already know we share a room.

"Hey! M-morning. Sorry." His face is mildly panicked, and it kills any joy I had. Not even his soaking wet body, all pressed up against me, can keep the disappointment away.

I don't know what this is or what's happening between us, but I know it won't last long. It can't. He has too much to lose, and I can't be a dirty secret. I've had too many of those in my life. Being one isn't an option.

"Are you okay?"

"Yeah. No, I'm fine. I'm getting dressed."

"Oh, okay. Sorry." She goes on about how she wanted to catch him before his test, and he doesn't stop trying to get his phone from me in between offering clipped replies for a couple of minutes. He does lose some of the fight when she brings up winter break, letting his wet forehead rest on my shoulder while she talks about whether or not he still plans on spending it with them. I guess the topic is safe enough for me to hear.

It feels deliberately rude of them both—even though she doesn't know I'm listening. I'm not a part of the family, and hearing about what I'm sure will be a happy holiday without me definitely cements that.

"So, you'll come down and spend the whole break with us, right?"

"Not the whole break, but most of it. I should work for part of it. We'll probably leave next weekend. I don't—"

"We? You *and* Nic?"

"Well... yeah?" He lifts his head, his face awfully close to mine as he stares at my reflection in the mirror before us. He looks mildly hopeful, like he wants me to go with him and is only just now wondering if I didn't plan on it.

But of course I didn't plan on it. Nobody fucking told me anything about it. And what does that even mean, that stupid look on his face? There's no way he wants to tell them about us and the mess we've haphazardly thrown ourselves into. So, then, what? He's so horny he can't handle a couple weeks without the easy access?

"I just didn't think he'd want to come," she speaks softly, clearly tiptoeing around her feelings on the subject.

It's quiet and uncomfortable. His fingers make a move for the phone again, but I'm not quite done. I'm proving a point. I know he thinks I'm the bad guy where our parents are concerned, but he doesn't see things from my perspective. The deliberate way they've *both* excluded me from things—even his precious mom.

I started a lot of it, but I was young. Young*er* and hurt. I was awful, but I've tried to mend things to no avail.

"He's coming." He sounds sure but doesn't look it.

There's a question in his gaze, but I don't know how to answer it. It depends—on her and him. On Anton and how much I'm willing to subject myself to—because do I really want to see them happy and whole while I sit somewhere on the sidelines alone? Plus, Cade did say work is pretty easygoing as far as college kids and their weird schedules go, but I just started. Taking time off may not be an option.

"Oh. Okay. That's good." All pretense ends with an unhappy droll in her next sentence. "I guess."

It's almost funny, the way Cade's face twists in confusion.

"Are you sure he wants to? He—if he doesn't want to come, don't press it, okay? I just got rid of him, and I really don't want—"

"Mom!"

This time, I let him take the phone out of my hand and watch him in the mirror as he leaves the bathroom. I should leave it, but I'm trailing after him only seconds later. He's still naked, standing there with his body on display as he politely argues about whether or not I'm going to their place for Christmas.

I don't even want to go. I'm not big on holidays— I haven't been since that last good one my mom and I had. But I don't know. It might be nice if someone wanted me there.

And it sounds like Cade does. At least he's trying to stand up for me. Maybe. Feeling somewhat worried about where it is I'd go if not to my dad's house. Maybe. Fuck, I can't really tell what the point of all this back and forth is.

I'm not used to seeing this. Someone wanting me around—that doesn't happen. So I can't be sure if it's real or something I'm reading too much into. It doesn't seem likely, even as he tells her that we can share his room—because while what was once my room is now full of her failed hobbies and shit, he does still have one.

"But Mom, he should be able to go to his dad's house for Christmas. Okay." He scoffs, his broad shoulders tensing to match the frustration in his voice. "What do you mean—vacation where?" He's quiet while she apparently tells him what the plans are—plans I don't get to hear. "Well, he's coming, so..."

I don't get it. My chest swells as he goes on, his voice getting quieter the more annoyed he gets. It sounds like he really wants me to go, but I don't fucking get it.

Until suddenly, I do. Thinking over the past week, I can guess. In a weird way—having to force the disappointment aside—it's calming. At least I'm not sinking in confusion anymore because, yeah, Cadence Howard wants my dick around on his winter break, and I can definitely deal with that.

I reach out to touch him, letting my hand barely skim over the swell of his ass before he's facing me in shock, stunned that I'd touch him while he's talking to his mom. I ignore their conversation and his panic as I reach for his flaccid dick, putting all my focus on that as it starts to stiffen in my hand even as he stutters through their talk.

"I don't—" his fingers circle my wrist, a hard beam in his eyes that makes me genuinely smile. He really is gorgeous—even when he looks at me like he wants to punch me. I've always begrudgingly thought so, but seeing him like this is next level. Cheeks rosy as his lips part on a silent breath, lust and anger so clearly painted in the green of his eyes. He's made jokes about me and glow-ups, but Cade didn't need to glow-up. Prettiest little whore there is.

"Mom, I have to go." But she keeps talking, and he keeps listening. She could be telling him anything—droning on and on about how moody and mean I am.

It's pure spite that has me sinking to my knees. Maybe it has a little to do with me not wanting Cade to have words about how awful I am being said in his ear, but mostly, it feels like spite. A big fuck you to Tracey in the form of me dirtying up the family's golden boy. Cade's gasp as I swallow him down, the way his hand curls in my hair, his hips bucking forward instead of away from me—all of that's just a bonus.

Cade wants me, and I'm pathetic for eating that up, but fuck. It feels good. His cock, hot and heavy on my tongue for the first time, feels like proof that there's someone who wants *me*. I'm exaggerating things, but not by much—lashes fluttering as I groan too loudly for his liking. But when he tries to tug on my hair to shut me up, I respond by groaning louder. I don't like things as rough as he does, but I like this. I'm apparently starved for it, being fueled by the throbbing in my groin and the look on his face as he watches me.

I gag on him, finally earning me a moan loud enough for mommy dearest to hear him, and he can't hang up fast enough. "Mom, I have to go—*fuck, Nic.*"

God. I love him telling her who it is that's got him all flustered. *Say my name, lover boy.*

"I'm sorry. Bye."

I pull off him with a slurp, wiping at the spit dripping down my chin.

"You think you're so fucking funny, don't you?"

"Not really." I smile, feeling happy with the very subtle ache in my jaw. "But I do think you should lay down."

"I—no. I have an exam."

"I'll be quick."

"Oh, well... as enticing as that is..."

"Why do we always have to do this? Play this little back-and-forth before I fuck you every single time—isn't it tiring by now? We both know you'll lay down for me, so let's skip all that."

"You—" His cheeks flush red in a renewed blush, his cock still bobbing in my face. "You look good on your knees."

"Yeah." I nod, just briefly playing into his attempt to deflect. "I'd look better inside you, though."

He huffs, but one look at his bed has him caving. "Whatever. Just—okay, but you do need to hurry." He crawls up, giving me my favorite view. "And not so much lube!"

We've had this argument a few times. I do go a little excessive on the lube, but he won't let me stretch him enough to make skimping an option. I've bottomed, and I know how much it can fucking suck, so too bad. "I'll use as much as I need to."

I have to use his bed to brace myself as I stand, suddenly grateful that he's given me his back so he doesn't have to watch me struggle. He has his hole on display just for me, and it's enough that I can ignore the way the band of my sweats feels on my legs.

I've thought about asking him if we can ditch the condoms, but I don't want to have that talk about exclusivity and shit. Especially not right now. He's never even looked at me while I've fucked him—if I didn't make him say name, I'd think he was imagining it was somebody else while I was inside him.

That doesn't have anything to do with condoms, but as I rush through prepping his ass, I can't help but think about it. It makes me mad wondering why he doesn't want to look at me, why he's always so careful to make sure I take him in this position only. He grunts as I move to three fingers, his hole spasming around them as I take my anger out on his insides.

"That's enough." His hips jerk, pushing back against my hand as I thrust inside him. "Nic, I'm ready," he mutters impatiently.

I pull my sweats down enough to free my cock, moving on autopilot as I slide the condom on and slather myself with lube.

"Nic," he scolds, shooting me a long-suffering glare over his shoulder. "That's too much. Wipe some off."

I ignore him and shove my fingers back inside him to try and get rid of some of the excess gel on my hand, quietly laughing when he moans. As soon as I'm notched right up against his loosened hole, he tries to push himself back, too needy to wait for me.

"Wait."

"No, hurry. Nic—"

"You should have a safeword."

"What?" His voice changes drastically, cutting through the haze he was sinking in. "No. That's stupid."

"You like shit rough, Cade. And you also like pretending you don't want me to rearrange your insides, all while moaning like a pornstar." *It has nothing to do with* me—but it's me who makes him fall apart, and it's my name that he moans in those moments. Doesn't stop him from telling me that he wants nothing to do with me, though. "Having a word will make it so I actually know when you mean *no*."

"No."

I snort. "That won't work. Pick a word."

"Nic, I don't want to. Just because I like it to hurt a little, doesn't mean that—"

"Fine." I sigh, digging around so I can think of a word myself. He's so damn stubborn. "Cherry. We'll use cherry."

"Ch—why? Where the hell did that come from?"

I shrug. "Cherry, because I was thinking about how I popped yours." I slide two fingers inside him, taking the time to rub more lube as deeply as possible just because I can.

"You didn't pop anything, asshole. I was *not* a virgin!"

"Hm." I laugh. "Yeah, that's true, but this ass wasn't

as ran through before taking my dick, little slut." I drag my fingers out, giving myself a stroke as I watch his hole close. I don't know why he won't admit it, but I know I'm right.

I don't care if he is a slut or not because it doesn't matter. He is one when my cock is involved. He's never once protested to me calling him that, and if anything, he enjoys it. I've been called similar things, have even let it happen, but it doesn't do for me what it does for my greedy boy. But having this safeword will let me know if I go too far.

"Also..." I want to see him. More than that, I want him to see me. If I'm not letting him pretend he doesn't want me anymore, then that should include him having to watch me as I fuck him. "Turn around," I tell him, forcing some authority in my voice. It's usually easy to come by with him, not at all something that needs effort. He's just so needy and hard up that he's more than willing to be bossed around when he's on his knees, but this command feels like a big deal. And the silence that fills the room tells me I was right to be wary. But I want him on his back. I fucking want him to look at me.

"Come on. On your back." I pat his hip, moving back so he can roll over.

"Why? We can—"

"You happily let me wreck your ass on a regular basis, but you don't want to look at me?" I scoff. "Turn around, Cade."

"What are you talking ab—"

I cut him off as I move him into place, pushing

until he's on his back and I'm able to fit between his legs.

"Dick," he breathes when I've got him positioned how I want. "Okay, damn. I didn't know you wanted th—*oh*," he groans, head falling back with a wince as I finally sink inside him. He grabs his thighs, pulling his knees to his chest to open himself up for me before I'm even all the way in. "*Fuck*," he whispers.

All the pleasure on his face almost surprises me. I don't give him time to adjust, going straight to fucking in and out of him after that first slow thrust. It's how he likes it, and I know that, but I assumed it would hurt him. And maybe it does, maybe that's the appeal. His jaw goes slack as I slow down a bit, watching myself in a daze as I disappear over and over inside the perfect heat surrounding me.

It's a struggle not to watch his face. I just can't believe that it's him beneath me—moaning on my cock. He bites his lips to hide a whimper, our eyes getting caught on one another as I slam into him harder and harder. "Stop staring." He moves a hand to the headboard to stop his head from hitting it, and I have to laugh.

"Can't help it. You're such a pretty little whore," I tease, aiming for that spot inside him that makes him sing.

"*Fuck*," he moans, reaching for his dick and sliding his precum down its length.

"Gonna come on your big brother's cock, Cade?"

"Ah!" he cries out, his legs wrapping around me in an attempt to pull me in deeper. He loves it when I talk like that—gets off on the taboo despite denying it any other time. He reaches for my hand, is clumsy with it as he leads me to his neck. When i finally give him what he wants, a firm necklace wrapped right around throat, he moans. "Oh, god."

"Not God." I lean in, moving my lips to his ear. "Tell God who it is making you feel this good, little brother."

"You—*oh, fuck.*"

"Who?" I thrust in hard enough to make him hiss, my balls slapping against his skin, tightening my hand just a bit.

"Nic!" His voice is raspy, my hold on his neck not quite tight enough to cut off too much air. His fingertips dig into the tops of my shoulders just as his ass squeezes around my cock with an impossibly tight contraction until I'm moaning into the bend of his neck. "So fucking good." His breathing picks up, coming out in a higher pitch as he gets closer. "*Nic,*" he whines, sounding wrecked. "More. Again."

I have to prop one of his legs up, move it over my shoulder so I can give him the violent thrusts he wants. The kind that make the bed move and tears swell in his eyes. He doesn't even realize that I've let go of his throat, he's so close he can hardly handle his own dick. I take over for him, stroking him in sync with the movements of my hips as I let my face hover above his. It's not much longer before I'm watching in awe as he throws his head back, cum spilling over his torso while he makes the ugliest face I've ever seen.

It looks so stupid it's almost endearing. I hate it.

I stop moving as soon as he's done, leaving him a

boneless, sweaty heap beneath me. The apples of his cheeks are bright pink, his hair a mixture of frizz and damp. It's wild that he can go back to being so sexy after making that awful O face.

"Please."

I know what he wants instantly. Cade hates it when he finishes first. He wants me to come—wants proof that he makes me feel good too—but he gets too sensitive pretty much the second his balls unload. Even now, he's fighting a cringe as I pull out.

"Nic, please."

I could tease him about this. I don't know why he's always so hung up on me coming, but he really is. Gets sad and needy for it until I do. That first time we fooled around, I didn't, and I think that bothered him —which I can sort of understand. So, I don't make fun of him for it. "Shh." I rub his thigh, trying to soothe him as I take the empty condom off. "I'm gonna come, Cade." I don't bother with more lube, choosing instead to run my hand through the mess he made on his abs so that I can stroke myself with his cum. He watches my movements hungrily, body writhing like it's his cock I'm touching.

"Your body is unreal."

I check his face, looking to see if he's telling the truth, and find him staring at me like he could go for round two right this second.

"Honestly." He gives me a sleepy smile as he trails a hungry look over my torso. "Fucking gorgeous. It's hard to believe you're that little emo boy I met all those years ago."

BRIANNA FLORES

Leave it to him to ruin the moment.

"You're still kind of emo, I guess. Broody little shit. You—"

"Do you want me to come or not?"

"Sorry, sorry." He laughs, not at all apologetic. "Stroke that big dick, emo boy."

"Cade." I stop all movements and stare up at the ceiling as he laughs.

"Okay, okay. Here, just…" He moves over, shoving his comforter off to the side. "Lay down."

I do as he says, letting him be the bossy one for once. I don't expect him to straddle me, but the way he gathers more cum off his body and grips me in a firm hold has me biting back any complaints. His hand is warm, a firm hold as he works my foreskin like a sleeve. It's not as good as being inside him, but his eyes fixed intently on me makes it worth it.

I try not to react too much when he starts singing me praises, but I love it. Eat it up as much as he does my attention because I think I need it in the same way he needs the things I give him. But I can't let him know that, so I keep quiet. Just enjoy it and commit it all to memory.

I don't last long, his focused touch pushing me back to the edge in just a few minutes. He makes sure my cum lands on him, painting his torso with the orgasm he's claimed—going as far as arching his back with a soft moan. He really is a bit of a cumslut. It's kind of… sweet, in a sick way.

"Damn." He lays down beside me, aggressively shoving hair off his forehead. "You look stupid when you come."

I watch him run his fingertips through the mess splattered across his six-pack, feeling all sorts of comfortable lying next to him.

"Well, you look beautiful when you come." He looks crazy in that moment—actually demented or dying—but it doesn't feel like a lie to tell him differently. He is beautiful. Always.

Sixteen

Cade

"**D**ude. You said you were going to come right at eight. That's the whole reason I showed up so early."

I don't tell him that the reason we agreed to come early is because *he* needed the extra time—there's no point in lecturing Liam about school. He does okay. He tries just enough to pass everything, but he's also been studying for a degree he has zero interest in, and that definitely shows.

And I definitely don't tell him why I was late. That's none of his business. He has an idea, has asked me how things are with Nic a few too many times to make me paranoid, but he doesn't *know*. And Nic might actually murder me if I blabbed.

"I still finished before you did." I finished early enough to see the messages from my mom and argue some more. I can't believe her. Nic is her stepson, and I know—I, of all people fucking know—how difficult he can be, but he's grown up some. He's not the same brat he was years ago. And he had his reasons to be mad—I may not know all of them, but I'm sure watching your dad fall out of love with your mom is tough.

Or maybe I'm blinded by all the orgasms. I do understand why my mom wouldn't be excited for him to come along—he doesn't like her, but still. Anton is his dad, and it's been years since he spent Christmas with us. He usually goes to his mom's, but he's already told me he has no plans this year—which our parents know. I didn't ask why, but I know that it's a big deal.

She's probably still blowing up my phone, but I do not care. I meant what I said. She sent me screenshots and links to a hotel in fucking Sedona and told me she and Anton booked three flights. Three! Why would Anton be okay with that?

This impromptu vacation is a big deal. I thought they were saving for a wedding, but apparently, she has the gist of that worked out. They're having the ceremony at a church near the end of winter break and were hoping for this to be their version of a honeymoon since they'll be working after the wedding. Most people would do it on their anniversary, but my mom is very excited. She secured the earliest date at the chapel she wanted.

I told her I would walk her down the aisle and that I was happy she was getting the wedding she wanted, but why do I need to come on their impromptu honeymoon? She can jazz it up as a family vacation as much as she wants—I told her I wasn't going unless Nic goes.

She must think that I'm bluffing, but I'm not.

That's why my phone is on silent. I don't care how much money they spent on the tickets, that's their problem. Not Nic's.

"Okay." Liam scoffs. "Fuckin' nerd."

I push the drama aside for the time being, deciding to live in the moment with Liam. I've missed this. It's not always this easy to be around him anymore, so I have to enjoy it when it is. "What are we doing now?"

"Well, I actually got a—ugh. Look at him in his slutty ass pants."

I follow Liam's glare to find Sebastian next to his Jeep—standing there in what we've both always dubbed some slutty ass pants. Well, they're just grey sweatpants, but everyone knows the deal with those. It reminds me of Nic—those are all he wears when he's at home. And I'm a simple bisexual man—I see grey sweats, and my eyes are involuntarily searching for a dick print. Like right now.

"Damn. For your butt's sake, I hope he's more of a shower than a grower."

"Shut up." Liam pushes at my shoulder, but it doesn't keep me from seeing the blush on his cheeks. "Don't look at his dick."

"It's kind of hard not to, Liam."

"Just—don't!" We get close enough for Sebastian to reach an arm out for Liam, and even though he moves in for the touch, eagerly pressing into Sebastian's side, he also turns his head to dodge a kiss. "I really wish you'd changed."

"Liam," he groans quietly, tossing his head back like someone who has for sure already had this argument. "They're just sweats!"

"Exactly! Even Cade said he can see your dick."

"That's—what? No, I was just—" I look around, trying and failing not to sneak another peak at Sebastian's crotch. It really is the pants. It's almost as bad as when Nic wears them. But Liam's bottoms aren't much better. "What about you, huh? You're wearing booty shorts in the middle of December." It doesn't snow here, but it's not exactly short-short weather either.

"Well, yeah, but—" He looks down at the khaki shorts stretched to the max across his thighs and shrugs. "I only wore these because of him. I would have changed if he had."

"We're not getting into this again." Sebastian even removes his arm from around Liam's waist, something I don't think I've ever seen him do. They're a very touchy couple—they don't pull *away*.

"I just don't think you need to hang out with Jax in pants like this, Bash. We all know he—"

"I don't want your stupid boyfriend!" Jax's head pops out of the passenger window, sneaking up on me in a way I wouldn't expect a yapper of his caliper to be able to. "He's like a brother to me, Liam—I've told you this. I joke and shit, but I do *not* want your boyfriend's stupid pierced dick!"

"A brother who you've fucked," Liam grumbles, tucking his face into his boyfriend's neck. Sebastian whispers something to him that has his neck flushing pink, and it feels a bit like I'm intruding all of a sudden. I don't know if it's the view or the topic of brothers fucking and pierced penises, but I'm very much uncomfortable. "Okay, well…" He finally comes up for air to speak directly to me. "We got to go. I have work soon, and I should probably change."

"Work?" This is news to me. Liam has never been a spoiled kid, but he does come from the kind of money that's ensured he's never had to work. "Since when? Where?"

"It's a secret." It's Jax who answers, his head still hanging out of the car.

"Why?"

But Jax is right. Liam doesn't want to tell me—even dodging the question has him once again blushing.

"Okay…" I shrug, feigning indifference. "I don't even want to know." I do, though. It bugs me that we're the kind of friends who have secrets. I know I'm not one to talk—having hidden a pretty colossal secret from Liam for years—but still. Why is his pampered ass working, and why would he be too embarrassed to tell me?

"Yeah, me either." Jax gets out of the Jeep so Liam can take his spot in the passenger seat. It's not until Sebastian gets in and starts the car that Jax lets us all know his plans. "And I don't want to go back to your place just so you can leave me with your little rat-dog while you diddle each other's peens. I'm going with Cade."

"Ugh," I whisper, but he doesn't believe in personal space and hears me.

"Oh, come on. You know you love me." He doesn't even ask me if I'm okay with lugging his ass around before he's heading for my car.

"I guess I'm hanging out with Jax."

"Sorry." But Liam's grinning like he's not at all sorry and maybe even happy that Jax isn't his problem for the time being. "He's not so bad. Just... keep him busy."

∞ ∞ ∞

"So, what do you want to do?"

"Take you home," I answer honestly, but he only rolls his eyes in response. I didn't actually think that would work anyway.

"We could hang around Seb's and follow Liam to work. I don't know why he's being so sketchy about that, but I've been meaning to follow him for a while now anyway."

"What—no. That's creepy, Jax."

"Oh, so stalking is only okay when it's your boyfriend?"

"I don't have a boyfriend." I leave it at that, simply not in the mood to elaborate.

"Okay, so your fuck buddy or whatever else you want to call him. Why can we stalk him but not Liam?"

"Jax, we're not following Liam to work. And we did not stalk Nic!" I really wish people would stop saying that.

"Well... do you *want* to stalk Nic?"

I stare at him for all of two seconds with my jaw agape before I throw my car in drive—the decision to drive to the diner fully formed. It's a bad idea, but it's too tempting, especially since I know where he is. I imagine it'd be hard to stay away from him, having that knowledge locked and loaded in my one-track mind. My thoughts are pretty consumed by Nicolas Aldana these days.

A part of me thought that getting his dick would cure me from this whole Dumb Dick disease I've got going on, but I was wrong. I was way wrong. If anything, my symptoms are worse. I pretty much think in terms of my broody emo boy these days. If I had ended up doing anything else, I still would have obsessively counted the hours until he was off.

"This is fun."

"No, it isn't." Honestly, it is. I feel a little giddy as we pull into the diner's parking lot. I know it's not a good idea, that he's going to be mad as soon as he sees me, but I don't know. I kind of like it when Nic is mad at me. It gets my heart pounding in a way that I can usually feel in my dick.

I don't know if Jax can handle that, though. A pissed-off Nic with Jax in reaching distance—it could be bad if I let Jax be all... himself.

"Hey, maybe don't talk to him. At all."

"Why?" He pouts, acting like he genuinely doesn't understand why I don't want him speaking to Nic.

"Just... don't."

"Don't you work here?"

"Yeah." I park in my usual spot right next to Nic's car. "So does Nic."

"Well... I'll have to talk to him to order my food. We are getting food, right?"

I didn't think about it before I brought us here, but that does seem like the most obvious choice— this being a restaurant and everything. It gives me an excuse to be here.

"Just tell me what you want, and I'll order for you."

"That seems unnecessary, but okay."

It's for sure necessary. I don't see a world where Nic can tolerate Jax.

It's not until we get inside that I start to feel nervous. I do like it when he looks at me like he wants to kill me—especially now that I've come to associate that look with his cock ripping my ass apart—but I don't know for sure how he's going to react to having to wait on me. Our hostess seats us in what I know to be his section, and he sees us as soon as we sit. I can tell because he immediately looks like he just stepped in some dog shit. The squishy kind. While barefoot.

Why do I like him so fucking much?

"He did *not* look happy to see you."

I glare at Jax, but he's too busy playing with the sugar packets on the table to notice. It's not until Nic walks over that he finally stops his fidgeting just to smile at my stepbrother. And if Nic is unhappy to see me, he sure as fuck isn't all that tickled to see Jax.

"What are you doing here?"

"I—" I shrug, feeling too exposed now that he's got

his attention on me. I underestimated how this would play out. Things aren't anywhere near lovey-dovey between us, but they're not quite this icy, either. I don't know how to play it now that I'm out of practice.

"Cade. Why are you here?"

"We wanted..." I don't know why I'm here. Or I do, but I can't tell him that. *I just wanted to see you.* That sounds like something I'd say post-lobotomy. I can't tell him that.

"Food," Jax cuts in and mouths a silent and very unsubtle *sorry* when I overreact to his voice. I probably needed the help, but I gave him very specific instructions.

"You could have gone literally anywhere else," Nic states the obvious, refusing to acknowledge Jax.

"But we didn't." I sit up straighter, deciding not to be a coward while he looks daggers at me. "Why does it even matter?" Honestly. Is Nic an asshole? Absolutely, but I don't see why he should be this pissed at me.

He stares at me for a beat before pretending that whole conversation didn't happen. He goes right into treating me like a regular customer—asking me what I want like he doesn't know I get the same thing here every day that I work when I'm on break. He even politely—sort of—asks Jax what he wants, but he didn't get a chance to tell me, so he ends up ordering for himself. The only difference between how he's acting now and how he treats the diners is that he usually fakes some smiles for them.

"Buddy, I don't know how to tell you this," Jax

starts as soon as Nic has left the table, and I already know he's going to say some bullshit. "But your boyfriend hates you."

"He's not my boyfriend." I feel those words in my chest, feel them squeeze uncomfortably tight around whatever dumb organ is in there.

"You know what? I believe you. We probably should have gone somewhere else. All the servers here are rude as hell."

The last time he was here, I was the one who waited on him and Sebastian. They were trying to ask me for ideas on where to take Liam for a date, and I *was* a little shitty to them. But so was he.

I can't get my mind off Nic—because of course I can't—so I get up.

"Hey, where are you going?"

"The bathroom," I lie, walking away quickly with hopes that he isn't someone who likes to join people on bathroom trips. I find Nic by the drink station and don't think before I'm letting a flat hand shove into his shoulder blade—not hard, but enough that he spills some of the drink in his hand. "What's wrong with you?"

He's not in the mood, might even be planning on trying to ignore me, but just as I'm about to really lose my shit, he turns around. "We're done."

"I—" My face falls, everything inside me following suit. I can feel my guts sinking right to the floor, that idiot heart of mine pounding on its way down. "Why? What do you mean? I—"

"I don't want to fuck you anymore, not if you're

193

going to be running around with whoever the fuck that is. We spent this morning in your bed, Cade, and now you're here with some other guy? I don't know who the fuck you—"

"No! I'm not—no. Nic, Jax is just... he's not even a friend. I told you that! He's just..." I stop talking, let myself catch my breath so that I can fix this. "Why would I bring a date or—"

It hits me that he's jealous right then, and the realization has my body short-circuiting. He's still fucking jealous of Jax—it's so ridiculous I almost want to laugh. If I weren't still reeling from him trying to end things, I might. Yeah, I can totally fix this.

"I'm not sleeping with Jax. I wouldn't bring a hookup to the place I work, Nic. Why would I do that?"

"I don't know—because you're a dick? I work here too, and you wanted me to see you with—"

"No." This guy. He's just as clueless as the rest of us. "Nic, I swear. Jax is nothing." I feel a little bad saying that—Jax is okay—but I have to convince Nic that he's not his competition. There is no competing with Nic.

"Why else come here?"

The look on his face isn't like anything I've ever seen, at least not on him. It reminds me of myself—of all the times I've felt vulnerable or insecure, only it's worse. It's *so* much worse seeing it on him. It makes me want to do something crazy.

Pretty sure it's given me that lobotomy I was dreading.

"I wanted to see you."

His brows raise, surprise wiping that sad look off

his face. I'm glad. It's worth the humiliation just to see him no longer looking at me like that.

The lobe of his ear is pale, the perfect shade to let me see it when he blushes. He's so pretty. He doesn't understand the hold he has on me. I'm not sure I do either.

He doesn't know what to say. I don't either, but I'm glad I was able to clear things up. He's not mad at me anymore and still standing close enough to me that I can feel his body heat.

I don't know which of us goes in first, but I'm so fucking ready to feel his mouth on mine. I hold my breath, don't even take the time to wet my lips, and begin feeling lightheaded just from the anticipation of it.

I'm going to kiss Nic.

There's so much excitement and eagerness bubbling inside me that I don't even realize he's not leaning in anymore.

"I gotta get back to work."

"Right." It feels like he just punched me in the gut. His rejection has always stung, but this is more. Worse. This feels like heartbreak.

Seventeen

Nic

"**G**uess what?"

"What?" I set my phone down beside me on the bed to enjoy the show. The first thing he does when he comes home from school is get naked. Well, he changes into more comfortable clothes, but getting naked is a step in that whole process—and it's one I usually appreciate.

"I said guess!"

"You... oh." I sit up fully, a little more proud of myself than I should be that I remembered. "You took your last final today."

He smiles at me, clearly also surprised that I remembered. It makes me feel good—seeing his smile. Pointed at me, even. Things have been a little awkward between us ever since I turned down his kiss. I still feel bad about it, but I couldn't embarrass myself. Not in front of him.

And honestly, it feels like a big deal. We don't kiss. Never have, and most of the time it feels like we never will. I almost gave in but I'm glad I held back.

Well, that's bullshit, but it's what I'm telling myself.

"Yup. I am officially done with this semester. We have work tomorrow, and then we go up to San Jose—"

"*You* go up to San Jose."

He pauses with his shirt half off for a second before quickly ripping it off. "Nic—"

"Cade, I don't want to go. How many times do I have to tell you that?" I'm tired of being around people who make it obvious that I'm not wanted there. That I'm taking up space I have no right to be occupying. And I haven't been to their house for the holidays in years. It's just been me and my mom, sometimes Paulina, my mom's only friend. It would feel weird to spend the day with my dad just because I can't spend it with her.

And Tracey *just got rid of me.*

"You said you didn't want to spend Christmas with our parents, but they won't be there."

I sigh, not bothering to get into this again. I did forget about that, but still. It's weird. And he can lie as much as he wants—I know this whole vacation business is only a thing because I'm in the mix.

"Nic, why don't you want to go with me?"

Truthfully, I do want to go with him. Thinking about what else I could do and who I could spend that day with, I always end up coming back to my mom or Cade—and only one of those is an actual possibility. He's it. All I've got. But I've learned a few too many lessons in life. If something sounds too good to be true, it usually is.

"I have to work. I need to save as much as I can before the spring semester starts." It's not even a lie —not a total lie. I have enough that I could afford to get in a place, but it wouldn't hurt to have more. A squirrel fund to keep me afloat when I no longer have roommates to help lighten the load—when it's up to me alone. So, yeah, if I want to move out of Cade's room, then I'll need more money.

Maybe he wouldn't be trying so hard to convince me to go if I told him that, but a part of me doesn't want to see him get excited to be rid of me. Not yet.

"Actually..."

"What?"

He's looking at me with barely veiled caution, sliding his jeans over his hips slowly as he watches my face.

"You're gonna be mad at me."

"I'm always mad at you."

He snorts, kicking his pants off the rest of the way before moving closer to my bed. "I requested time off for you."

"You—how? Is that even allowed?" Pretty sure there are laws about that kind of thing. Plus, I saw the schedule a few days ago. I'm on it.

"I don't know." He shrugs, fidgeting with the edge of my bed as he stands there in his briefs. "I just told him we both needed the time off, and he gave it to us."

"I... I'll tell him my plans changed and that I can work."

"No!" My bed bounces under his weight as he flops

down. "I don't want to go alone, Nic."

I didn't even think about that. I don't get Anton and Tracey. He's supposed to be the favorite, so why didn't he get an invite to their fancy destination vacation? And why am I letting it be my problem? "What about Liam?"

"He'll be with his boyfriend this year."

"Cade… you don't want to spend your Christmas with me."

"Clearly, I do!" He stands up again, his dumb muscles tensing with his frustration. "Why else would I ask a million times?"

He has asked a lot, that's true. He's asked so much I'm pretty sure *both* of us are tired of it. But it's not because he actually wants me to go. He just feels bad for me.

"Look, I'm sorry my mom is… I'm sorry. But I want you to come."

"You don't have to apologize for your mom, Cade. I doubt I'd be comfortable around my affair partner's kid either."

"You—what? What do you mean?"

I stare at him for a moment, his confusion mirroring my own. "You didn't know?"

"My mom and your dad… they had an affair?"

I nod, not bothering with more. I had no clue he didn't know that. I don't see it changing much of anything now that he does, though.

"I—god. What the fuck? My mom—no wonder you hate her!"

I laugh at that. But, yeah. No fucking wonder. Well,

that and the shitty attitude she tries hard to hide.

"I have no clue what to say. You're mom—"

"There's nothing to say, Cade." It's not his fault—something I've only recently begun to realize.

He nods his head, understanding that my mom is off limits. "But they won't be there, Nic. Just... please come with me."

But I don't budge.

"Whatever." His voice drops, the disappointment making him bitter. "I'll... see what Jax is doing, I guess."

I roll my eyes. He's only saying that to piss me off —I know this, but if anything, I'm more mad that it works. I don't know that guy, but I'm tired of seeing him and Cade together.

"Okay." I'm calling his bluff. He's done his best to convince me that he's barely even friends with Jax, and after everything he's told me, I do believe it. Which means he's full of shit right now.

It's not the reaction he wanted.

"I will."

"Okay." This time, I smile a little—can't help myself. He's just cute sometimes.

"Okay," he parrots me, his cheeks getting hot the longer he takes trying to come up with his next move. "I'm gonna call him. Right now."

"Tell him I said hi."

He grabs his phone off the dresser, and a few taps later, he's actually fucking calling him.

"Hang up." I move a foot to the floor, getting ready to do—something, I don't know.

"No. Hey! Um, no thanks. I just wanted to see if—"

We both stare at his phone where it lands on the ground—having been smacked out of his hand.

"It was Domino's."

"What?"

"I don't actually have Jax's number." He grins like he's proud of himself, and I can do nothing but stand here like an idiot. "So I called Domino's."

"Oh."

He wants to laugh at me but smartly decides not to. "Nic, please come with me."

My temple twitches as I stare at his pleading face. "You're giving me a headache. I *don't* want to."

He looks pained, like me actually rejecting his pity offer has hurt his feelings. I don't get it—truly do feel the beginnings of a headache. It hasn't been long since I got rid of the withdrawal symptoms quitting my meds caused, and I'm really not in the mood for any of them to make reappearance.

"I'm not having sex with you anymore unless you go."

He's full of shit. "Fine."

"Fine?"

"You're lying." I shrug.

"No, I'm not. Even if you say yes, I'm not letting you fuck me until we get there."

"You're—"

"I'm not kidding, Nic! No more ass for you."

This time, I'm less inclined to call his bluff. He might be serious. Sex benefits him just as much as me —more than me, probably. He initiates way more than

I do, so I don't really see how denying me his ass is a punishment for me alone.

Unless he actually does want me to go. At the diner, he told me that he was stalking me because he wanted to see me, but I'm still not sure that I can believe that. And even if he did mean it, I rejected his kiss just a minute after that—which seems like the kind of thing that would make someone regret pouring their heart out like that. But now this…

It feels risky to agree—feels like I'm potentially going to embarrass myself. But how bad could it be?

Worst-case scenario, I'm not alone for Christmas. Best case…

I swallow back my nerves—along with all the self-doubt that makes it impossible to believe him—and do something for myself. "Okay, Cade." My stomach tightens—whether with excitement or regret, I don't know—and his face lights up, making it so much easier to deal with. "I'll go with you—if…" I take a step closer and put a hand on his hip in a soft touch, reveling in how right it feels when he leans in, his chest against mine. "We fuck right now."

Cade hisses, baring his teeth as he shakes his head at me. "That wasn't the deal, emo boy. No ass for you until—"

I flip us, rearrange our bodies so that I'm able to shove him on the bed closest to us. He lands on his back with a full belly laugh, head thrown back as he props himself up on his elbows.

It has me pausing—standing and staring at him just so I can commit the image to memory. He looks so happy, and every part of me perks up—starts chanting the word *mine* over and over as it takes credit for the scene before me.

∞∞∞∞

"**D**id you bring lube?"

He gives me a side eye that tells me I was stupid to even ask such a thing. "Of course."

"And they're not going to be there?" I've asked maybe three or four times just since we got in the car, but I have plans—plans that would play out disastrously if our parents ended up being home.

"They're in Arizona." He has more attitude when he says it this time around, but I have to make sure. He'll understand later. See that it was worth it to humor me.

I hope he thinks it was worth it. I feel like I know him relatively well by now, so I really do think that he will, but that does fuck all to ease my nerves. My palms are a little sweaty—or a lot sweaty—but I'm going for it.

"Tired of the blue balls, huh?"

I don't give the cheeky bastard the satisfaction of a response—he's been way too proud of himself the past few days. I honestly didn't think he had it in him. If anyone else had told me my greedy little cumslut could go a whole week without coming, I'd have laughed in their face—but here we are, both of us experiencing new levels of horny. I really underestimated just how spiteful he could be—a mistake I will never make again.

And I *am* tired of the blue balls. It's what inspired the pervy idea that I'm beyond excited *and* nervous for. It's pretty much the only thing keeping my mind off missing my mom too much.

"Are you upset you didn't get to go to Sedona?" I might be if I were him. He's not used to being excluded from things. A tiny part of me is mad at them on his behalf, but most of me is happy with how things worked out—that it's just me and him.

Nic and Cade, Cade and Nic. Us. Ugh. I hate myself, hate how much I like that. *Us.* But, fuck, I really do.

"Nah. If I had a choice—red rocks or having my stepbrother come in my ass—I'd definitely choose the cum in my ass."

I don't know what to say—mostly because I know he's joking and wish he wasn't. I know he said he would choose cum, and that's not anything to feel special about, but it almost sounds like he'd choose me. I can't think of anyone ever choosing me before. Not once, not when it mattered.

But I don't let myself feel too important—he's just looking forward to ditching condoms. He was the one to bring it up. We had a brief and only mildly awkward discussion about STI screenings and PrEP—which he apparently is on—and agreed that we were good to go.

"Are you okay?"

The question catches me off guard, but it's instinct to tell him that I'm fine. He's not the only one who's been asking me that lately. I think he's probably asked the least—and since I spend most of my time with him, I figure that it's a good indicator that there's nothing to worry about. I'm feeling a little down, but I miss my mom, and that's normal. So, I stick with fine.

"Okay." He says it like he doesn't believe me and with the same look my old therapist used to give me when I'd tell her the same thing. But I am fine.

"I'm just tired." I've been feeling tired a lot lately, but it's to be expected. I have anxiety. Nothing major anymore, but I quit taking my pills, and I expected some drawbacks. Feeling anxious after going through a period of being somewhat decently well-adjusted is taking some getting used to. And things are more than manageable when it's just Cade and I.

We have less than an hour to go when I pull over at a rest stop. It's more time than a guy who prefers minimal prep needs, but he doesn't usually stretch himself and I want him to play a part in choosing how this whole thing will play out.

"Why'd you stop? We're almost there."

"You have thirty-two miles to get your ass ready for me."

"What?"

"Finger fuck yourself until you think you can handle me because as soon as we pull into the driveway, I'm going to give you a thirty-second head start, and then I'm coming for you."

"I—are you serious?"

If it weren't for the excited little gleam in his eyes, I'd backtrack, but I know him. I know how to make him feel good. He wants it rough, wants to be taken. Fucked to the point of pain, but only if it's mixed with pleasure. He asks for *more* every single time I'm inside him, but I hold back. I always give him just enough.

This is a promise for some of that *more* he craves.

"You've made me wait days, little brother. I'm going to fuck you whether you're ready for me or not." It's not true. I'd never do that, but I keep a straight enough face that he licks his lips before swallowing, liking the idea more than I'd like. I almost regret even saying that, giving him ideas.

He's quick to get out of the car, moving even faster to round the trunk. I pop it for him, and a few seconds later he's getting in the back seat.

"Other side." I want to be able to see his face, watch him as he works himself open for me.

"What if someone sees me?"

"Cade, the first time you choked on my dick, we were in a room filled with people."

"That's—" He purses his lips. "Different. That was different. Those people were doing nasty shit in a dark room. These people—" He motions towards the road with a jerk of his head. "They're not expecting to look over and see a guy with his fingers up his ass."

I laugh at that. Nobody's gonna see that, but I shrug anyway. "Oh well." I'm showing more confidence than I feel, but he's eating it up. Loving the risks involved and playing into it perfectly. It makes me wonder what kinds of people he hooked up with before me. Mostly girls, I'm sure. Did he act like this with them?

I hope not. I like thinking it's me. Being the one to open new doors for him—forcefully shove him over the threshold—makes me feel like I have a claim over this part of him. I may not have all of him, but the part of him that's dying to be fucked and ravaged is all mine.

I can hear him undo his zipper, the faint sounds of him shoving his pants down enough to give himself the room he needs. I can see him in the mirror, looking lost as he eyes his lap.

"Spread your legs, Cade. Put a foot on the center console."

He blows out a breath, a charming mix of nerves and relief on his face as he pulls his pants down more so he can do as I said. The snick of a cap sounds while I watch the road, and a quiet "*Shit*" follows. "I got a little lube on the floorboard. Or—it might be a lot." He gives me an apologetic grin and shrugs. "But you know, it could be worse. It could be nachos. My car still smells like fucking cheese." He tries to chuckle, but it comes out awkwardly.

"Cade, put a finger up your ass and shut up." The way his brows fall and settle in a little glare makes me smile. He's nervous, but it can't be any worse than when I prep him. Nine times out of ten, he rushes me and demands that I start with two fingers so he feels the stretch the way he likes. "I believe in you," I tease.

The next view I get in the rearview mirror is his

eyes closed in a subtle cringe, his bottom lip trapped between his teeth. I have to balance between watching his face and the traffic, but I get to see it when his mouth opens in a soft gasp. If it were my fingers, he'd be a lot louder. He'd already be working his hips against my prodding, eager for me to hit that spot inside him.

"Tell me how it feels."

His eyes open, cheeks painted a pretty shade of pink as he takes a breath. "Um…" His voice wavers, a sweet hint of those nerves that makes me wish I was back there to help him. "It's better when you do it." But a second later he's tilting his head back, still not quite moaning for me but definitely enjoying it. I have to adjust in my seat to try and alleviate the pressure on my growing erection. "Nic, I—you won't stop, right? You—" The word catches on the first audible sound of pleasure—a delicate groan that I feel in my groin. "I want you to fuck me, even if I say no."

This isn't some big surprise. "You want me to force my cock into you, make you take it." It wasn't a question, but he nods anyway. I have to push the heel of my palm into my groin to give myself some relief. "That's what I had planned—and you have a safeword."

"Ugh. Don't ruin it."

I laugh. He still very much resents me giving him one. It breaks the fourth wall of these little games we play to remind him that his no's don't mean anything, but that's too bad. I'll hurt him as much as he wants, but I won't do anything to push his boundaries.

Nearly twenty minutes of playing with himself has his breathing picking up, louder than the radio as he pants behind me. He's having too much fun, making it real fucking difficult to sit still. My dick is hard enough that it hurts. I may be speeding, but it's a necessity at this point.

I have to step hard on the brakes when I get boxed in, making him gasp as he's forced forward in his seat.

"Fuck, Nic. Don't do that."

"You need to stop." He's had enough time, and I'm not sure I can drive like this for much longer. I might end up just pulling over on the side of the road to fuck him now. "We're almost there," I say it for myself, a reminder that my suffering is nearly over.

Eighteen

Cade

I don't listen to him, feeling too good to stop touching myself. Plus, I don't know. Maybe he'll get mad at me.

I hope he means it—that he'll force me. Chase me and hunt me down. I have no clue what's wrong with me, why I crave the things I do but I have a hard time not blaming Nic.

His hate just feels so fucking good. He's sexy. He's extra sexy when he's pissed and when he's fucking me? I've technically only gotten to see it once—when he made me lay on my back—but he straight up wrecks me. The fucker glares when he comes—how hot is that? The answer is very. And he's rough and bossy and pretty much everything me and my Dumb Dick could ask for.

I read Twilight in high school—a secret I'll take to the grave—and I've been thinking about that sparkly bastard a lot lately. Specifically when he said that he was an addict and Bella was his own personal brand of heroin. I feel that shit in my bones. Only instead of a pretty Mormon-coded emo girl, my addiction is a pretty Eeyore-coded emo boy who can't stand me half the time.

I let out a moan that has him groaning through gritted teeth.

"*Cade*," he warns, but the sound of his voice only makes me hotter.

I have to wrap my hand around my dick again to give myself a few relieving strokes before letting go once more. I don't want to come until he's the one making me.

The only reason I do stop is because we're pulling off the interstate, finally taking the exit that leads to my mom's. I had to basically undress, leaving me looking stupid in just my shirt and socks—not that it wasn't worth it. I'm pretty excited, tucking my cock away with a familiar giddiness swirling in my guts that I can't shake. I pat my pocket to make sure my keys are where I need them, specifically feeling for my old house key.

"What if I don't get the door unlocked in time?"

"Then I guess we'll be giving the neighbors a show."

I can't decide if I believe him or not. I don't even hate the idea of it—if I wasn't sure it was against the law or, worse, that it would get back to our parents, then I might go for it. It's my kind of crazy—the kind that makes my blood pump straight to my cock. The same kind of crazy Nic is.

I watch those white strands of hair on the back

of his head as we drive down the street, now only seconds away from parking. He's so... everything. Infuriating and soothing, all wrapped up in a beautifully damaged package.

I want to kiss him. I don't know why he's so against it, but I need it. I want it so badly I've even dreamed about it a few times. His lips on mine, the way we'd fight for control until he'd grab me and forcefully take it—I want that.

"Nic?"

As soon as he looks at me with those grey eyes of his I lose the courage to ask him about it. He waits patiently for me to say something, cocking that half-white brow in a silent question, but I struggle with finding the words. By the time I think of something to tell him, we're already pulling into the driveway.

"Make it hurt." I throw the door open, slipping a bit on all the lube I spilled as I step out of the car and just book it for the door. I don't know if he meant it when he said he'd fuck me wherever he caught me, but it rings in the back of my mind loud enough that I decide the back door is the safest option.

The more distance I put between us, the more afraid I begin to feel. My focus is so zeroed in on what I'm doing that everything feels both sharp and hazy at once, and the second I begin to grapple with the lock, it only gets worse. That excitement is still there, sitting just above my groin and pushing me to move faster, but the very real threat of my stepbrother's dick is more prominent.

I hear the car door slam and let out a panicked

whimper, the stupid key finally turning being my only saving grace. The gravel on the side of the house is crunching under his shoes just as I bolt through the door.

I run through the kitchen to get to the stairs, happy when I make it without hearing him behind me. It feels like there are more steps than I remember there being as I take them two or three at a time, but I'm almost there. My room is—

"*Fuck!*" It's the only word I manage before the air is knocked out of my lungs, my chest hitting the edge of the top step making it impossible to breathe—to do much of anything, really. There's a buzzing sound in my ears as my body tries to recover, and the next thing I'm aware of outside of that noise is my jeans being dragged over my hips. I try to kick behind me only to end up with my knee pressed roughly against the wood with a thud.

"*Nic*—" My voice is raspy, and somehow, amidst all the fog, it reminds me of him choking me—of how good that shit feels, how empty it makes my head. "Nic," I try again, this time clearer, more desperate.

"My name sounds so fucking good on your lips, little brother."

I whimper, reaching for the rug lying in the middle of the hallway and not quite able to touch it. He has more leverage—on top of me while I struggle helplessly beneath him. It feels like I'm in danger, but just below all of that—the panic and distress—I know that I'm okay. That I'm safe. Nic only hurts me because I like it—most of the time. I trust him more than I ever thought possible, and I know he'll take care of me.

But the adrenaline is real.

"Tell me you want it, and I'll go easy on you."

"No!" I don't mean to sound so whiny, but no. He promised me some things, and I'm holding him to it. I don't want easy. The way he jerks my hips back, putting me in position for easy access right here on the staircase—that's what I want. I want Nic. I want—

Oh, fuck. I lay my sweaty forehead flat on the ground, unable to process anything but pain. I *almost* regret not going past two fingers and pouring more lube on Nic's floorboard than on my fingers. There's no getting used to this, that first punishing thrust—it always takes my breath. There's no time to get used to the invasion, just an instant state of being fucked. It feels hot, like he's searing my insides with every thrust he gives me.

And then it's not just pain. It's everything. It's me and Nic. Our moans are all wrapped around each other, literal music to my ears as he wraps his hand around me.

"*More*," I beg. I don't even know what more I could want—I just know I need it. More of him, of his dark little laugh he's breathing into my ear. It's all so, so fucking good.

"My greedy little whore." His voice is saturated in devotion—so much care and adoration in those words. *His* greedy little whore—fuck. I love that, him claiming me. His teeth graze my earlobe, forcing a needy whimper out of my mouth. "Turn around."

He pulls out too fast, a move that has me crying

out the split second I feel his absence. I try to do as he says, but my body is too stiff to cooperate—I need his help. He's aggressive as he gets me how he wants me —pulling my shoes and pants off all the way so he can fit where he's needed. My back hurts in this position, but he's lining up and sinking back into me, and it's all worth it. He holds my legs apart, a hand under each knee as he rocks inside me without mercy.

I think the word at times, those first few moments are borderline unbearable sometimes, but it always gets better. I'll never utter that stupid safeword he forced me to have. I can't imagine saying no to him and meaning it, not in these situations. I need him too much.

It feels like a small forever of this. It's brutal. Uncomfortable and painful but so, so good.

"I'm close, Cade," he groans, the tendons in his neck pulled tight as he strains, his pale grey eyes already fixed in that glare I'm so fucking gone for.

I reach for myself with a clumsy hand, but I'm closer than I thought, spraying endless ropes of cum after just a few tugs. The arm propping me up falters, making me slip down a step and forcing his cock deeper. He says something that I can't hear over my own cries of ecstasy, and I don't have the mental capacity to worry about it. It feels too good to stress about all the many bruises I'm for sure sporting, all the bullshit going on in my everyday life. Unrequited feelings, parents, Nic's moods.

Those are all things to dwell on later.

Right now I just want to feel good. Hollow in

a freshly washed sort of way. Almost weightless. Almost perfect.

"Nic?" My head feels heavy as I lift it to look at him.

"I know, baby." He starts to ease out, being gentle with it now that I've finished, but that's not how I need this to work. I manage to hook one leg loosely around him, hoping he gets the message. "I'm gonna come, Cade. I have to, but let's go to your room. I—"

"No, now. In me." There's a very real chance that I'll be mortified by this later, but at the moment, nothing else matters. "Come inside me."

He stares at me for a moment and waits until I'm close to begging again before he starts moving—this time slowly. Grinding his hips into me in steady rolls as he stays watching my face.

"Nic?" I bite my lip to hide a wince, oversensitive and uncomfortable despite all the tenderness.

He leans over me, his forehead pressed against mine, and it's exactly right for what I want.

"Please?" I whisper, too afraid to speak louder.

I feel his breath on my lips and see the indecision on his face as he realizes what I'm asking for. My arm slips under his so I can grab him, grip his shoulder in a fit of desperation. *Please. Please just kiss me.*

But he doesn't. He holds back, and it's awful. It ruins every bit of perfect the rest of today was. Absolutely shatters it. I'm so disappointed, and all I can do is let my head fall back and close my eyes. I won't cry, but I could.

His hand cups the nape of my neck, and maybe he wants me to look at him again, but the moment has passed. Rejection stings, but it's worse coming from him. I knew better, and still let myself hope. I feel so stupid.

And then his lips are on mine. They're chapped and timid and not at all like what I imagined. But he's kissing me, pressing his entire body on mine on what is easily the worst thing I've ever had sex on. There's no meeting of tongues. It's just his lips slowly moving against mine, and I'm so fucking in love with the feel of it that it hurts.

His orgasm is what breaks the kiss, but he doesn't go anywhere. Grunts a soft "*Fuck,*" against my lips before going still. I run my fingers through his hair and grin, forcing myself to hold in my gratitude. It feels like a moment of silence, a short time to process everything is needed, but he's moving out and off of me only seconds later.

It's for the best. My body has been through it. He helps me stand up, makes sure that I make it up the remaining steps, and still doesn't back away. He just lets me use him for support and leads me to my old bedroom. It's not until he tugs the comforter on my bed back that I recognize this behavior as something unlike him.

But I'm not complaining.

He's very gentle with me as he helps me out of my shirt—stopping to examine the bruises I'm very proud to wear. He asks if they hurt, but they don't. It's an ache, a dull soreness that I'll miss when it's gone.

When he disappears, leaving me lying on my stomach fully naked, I try not to be sad. But it feels a bit like I'm slipping. With my drug of choice gone, I'm left dealing with the comedown all by myself.

I flinch when something warm and wet is pressed over my hole.

"Are you okay?"

I feel silly for thinking he left me after all of that, but I am okay. Now I am. I nod my head to let him know and give him a tired smile to really convince him. I'm so much better than okay.

"I just need to grab our things. I'll be right back, okay?"

I make myself nod again—shove the clingy part of me that wants to tell him not to leave me away. I can still feel the withdrawal. It's not as bad as it was, but I hope he hurries.

∞∞∞

There's a gentle prodding at my entrance, something cold being rubbed into my skin.

"Better?" It's Nic's voice, his fingers working something soothing inside me.

I give him a drowsy moan, trying hard not to doze off again. He took longer than I expected. Either that, or I've been out for longer than it seems. "It feels nice," I murmur, trying to open my eyes only to fail completely.

"It should help with the pain."

"You'll sleep here, right—with me? You'll stay?"

"I—yeah. If you want me to."

I sigh dreamily, burrowing into the pillow under my face just as he drags his fingers out of me. He's rubbing more in random spots on my back and legs—areas that I assume are bruised. "Thank you."

I hear him huff a quiet laugh, his palm skimming over the back of my thigh. "You wouldn't even need it if it weren't for me."

"No, not—I mean, thanks for coming with me." I yawn, cozy enough that I know I won't have any trouble passing out. "I'm glad you're here, Nic." This time, I manage to peel my eyes open enough to look at him over my shoulder, but it's difficult. My head is heavy, and leaving it on the pillow is too comfortable. But I want him to know I mean it, so I reach with my hand, feel until I find his, and give him a squeeze. "Thanks."

His lips press against mine, a short and sweet little peck that has my mouth tugging into a sleepy smile. "Thank *you*."

It's the last thing I hear before I fall back to sleep.

Nineteen

Nic

No amount of lidocaine cream is helping the burn in my thigh. The shower didn't help no matter what temp the water was, and I'm not sure if massaging it is doing anything. I'm dreading standing up. Between the car ride and hunting Cade down, my legs are fucking tired.

I don't want to wake him up. I know that I do sometimes when this happens back at the apartment, but it's not because I want to. The bathroom door being in our room makes it hard not to disturb him, but my scars are off-limits, so he never says anything. We both know they're here, that they're ugly, and they hurt me, but we don't acknowledge it.

That's okay. I don't want him bringing it up, looking at them like he did the first and only time he saw them.

I wish, for close to the millionth time, that I hadn't fucked myself up.

But there's no point in wishing for things that

aren't possible. I'm probably going to sleep—*try* to sleep—on the couch downstairs. Or in the family room. I typically avoid that room because of Tracey, but she's not here. She's not at home with her son for the holiday, and I'm pretty sure that I'm the reason.

Or maybe I'm back to wishing for the impossible. Cade picking me—choosing to spend time with me over them—doesn't seem likely. I'm more of a last-resort kind of guy.

A wince has me giving up—digging the heel of my hand in my leg is doing fuck all for the pain anyway. I need some sleep. First, I have to get up and then get dressed. Walk down the hall past Cade's room where he's lying all bruised and battered and happy about it —like the pain slut he is. Right there in the same spot he was when he asked me to stay with him. It all seems like too much. Every step on the list requires so much effort—especially walking *past* Cade.

I don't expect him to barge in, especially since I thought I turned the lock, but there he is—with his bed head and bloodshot eyes and absolutely no decency. He's standing there in his birthday suit while I pull my towel off the ground to cover my lap. I'm still sitting on the edge of the tub, not a shred of dignity in sight.

"You said you'd stay."

The little frown on his lips has my chest pinching, something eerily close to affection warming my insides. "I'm in the bathroom, Cade."

"Well…" He shuffles on his feet, averting his eyes now that he's noticed my nakedness. "Are you okay?"

I can say I'm fine, almost do, but he won't believe me and I don't want to see the skepticism on his face. So, I say nothing.

"Wait here."

It doesn't occur to me that I didn't have to listen to him until I'm watching his flaccid dick bounce with his every step. It makes me laugh. "You could have put some shorts on."

"And deprive you of this view?"

"Looks like a dead fish."

"*Tsk*. You just wore him out." He holds up a round container wrapped in a black label for me to take. "It's my mom's. She gets it from the dispensary."

"CBD creams don't do much for me." Plus, it's hers. I highly doubt she'd be okay with me using it.

"It has CBD *and* THC. And it's the good shit that you can only get with a medical card."

I'm not convinced, and the look on my face tells him so.

"Just try it." He twists the cap off and shoves his fingers in the jar, scooping out a big glob and immediately sinking to his knees in front of me.

"I can do—*Cade*."

He ignores me, doesn't even ask which leg it is that's bothering me before he starts rubbing the cool ointment right into my scars. "How'd you do this? They're mostly uniform—like grill marks almost. Except this one. This is the one that hurts all the time, huh?" He looks up at me under his lashes, giving me a very brief view of his green irises. I used to tell myself his eyes were ugly. Compare them to muddy swamps or whatever else I could think of to try and convince myself that Cade isn't stunning. But lying to myself didn't change reality.

He pays more attention to me than I'd have guessed. Or maybe I don't hide shit as well as I think because how does he know this is my problem leg?

"*Ah*—" I go to grab his wrist as he digs his thumbs deeper into my mangled flesh, but hold back.

"Sorry. It should help, though."

"They were craft bars," I say after a moment of quiet, this time avoiding his eyes when he looks up at me. "My mom had these little brass rods, and I..." I shrug. There's no need to state the obvious. I'd take a lighter and wait until they were hot, and then brand myself—the evidence is right in front of us. Right where it always is, where I'll never be able to forget about them.

I don't know why I did it that way. I could have cut myself like a normal person. Hit myself and ended up with no scars. I don't know why I chose to burn my skin, but I know that it made me feel better. Sitting down, walking, doing anything that stretched the skin while I was simply struggling through my days also helped. It grounded me and gave me something to focus on other than how bad things were getting. Until I went too far. "This one got infected. That's why it's so much worse than the rest." It even needed a skin graft.

He hums his acknowledgment, going silent as he finishes rubbing the cream in. I wish I knew what he was thinking right now. If he thinks I'm an idiot for burning myself, he's not showing it. He seems focused, working my muscles with skilled fingers and saying nothing. He also doesn't look grossed out, so that's good. He wasn't at all bothered to touch me.

And when he's done, he smiles like a dope, jumping right into character like the perv he is. "You know what else is good for pain management?" He waggles his brows, and just in case that isn't enough of a hint, he pokes my dick.

"That's the sexiest way I've ever been propositioned for a blowjob in my life."

"Whatever." He scoots closer, taking me in hand and giving me a self-satisfied smirk when I start to stiffen. "It's not supposed to be sexy. It's for medicinal reasons."

I don't tell him that I already feel better, that just him being here has helped take my mind off of the pain. It's a selfish thing, letting him work me over like this, but I want it. It seems that I'm as starved for attention as he is.

He watches his movements closely, his bottom lip trapped between his teeth until I'm heavy in his palm. As soon as he decides I'm ready, he leans forward only to stop altogether.

"Hold on." He moves to get up, but I grab his shoulder to stop him, brow cocked in a silent question. "I need—" A nod at the sink clues me in. "My mouth is dry."

I don't think too hard about it before I cup his cheek, letting my thumb smooth over the stubble along his jaw and urging his face closer to mine. No words are needed as I lean down. If he were someone else, I might ask permission. But with Cade, there's no need. My stepbrother is always ready for whatever I want to give him.

He opens his mouth eagerly, the word cherry nowhere on his mind as his tongue extends over that pouty bottom lip of his. I can't help but lick, a swift run of my tongue over his—just to try it out—before I'm spitting in his mouth and listening to the faintest moan he's ever given me, so quiet I'd have missed it if I weren't so close to him.

He always starts by licking around the head, coaxing the foreskin back just enough so that he can fit the tip of his tongue beneath it. It's an intense feeling, one that makes my hips flex as I fight the urge to thrust. His eyes are closed as he sucks me into his mouth, swift little circles being smoothed over my frenulum driving me crazy—such a contrast to the otherwise gentleness.

He takes his time, massaging my balls as he slowly bobs his head lower and lower. Cade enjoys giving head. He approaches it like it's a gift—one he's always wanted. He hollows his cheeks eagerly, looking up at me as he sucks hard enough that I can't hold back. I thrust, the movement almost involuntary, but he doesn't seem to mind. Of course he doesn't. He wants to be used, wants to please.

"Greedy boy," I murmur the words softly, sifting my fingers through his hair as a pleasant warmth spreads throughout my chest. I adore him. He's annoying and immature and the only part of my days that I enjoy all at once.

I have to look away, look at the ceiling as I moan so I don't get too carried away with all this affection poisoning me. "*Fuck.*" It's overwhelming. Too fucking good. "Cade..."

He pulls off with a slurp, stroking me to soothe the absence of his mouth—one hand wrapped around me and the other gently kneading my sac. "Let's go back to bed."

"Cade," I start to complain, but he's already standing up, literally dragging me by the balls and giving me no choice but to follow him. There's some bruising along his lower back, a thick reddish-purple line that fans out and fades along the edges. Probably from the stairs. There's a few more, smaller and darker on his hip that I have to assume are from my fingers.

I feel a sick sense of pride as I take inventory of all the imperfections I've painted across his flawless skin. Discolored patches that remind me of my own, only prettier.

He should always be covered in my marks.

I don't ask as he leads me to the bed. It's usually him on his back or knees, but I make myself comfortable and wait for him as he grabs lube from where I placed it in his pack after he fell asleep. It's not until he's positioning himself over me, his solid frame straddling me, that I realize what he's doing.

"Cade, stop."

"I know, I know." He uncaps the lube and pours some directly on my cock, coating me in enough that I know he's doing it for my benefit because it's much more than he'd prefer. He's awkward with it as he attempts to line us up, but I'm stopping him again. "I'm good, Nic. Promise."

I let him sink down and have to grit my teeth as he does it. I love his mouth, the view, and the perfect wet heat—I fucking love it. But this is ten times better. His ass wrapped so tightly around me, his thick thighs pressed along the outside of mine.

"God, Nic. You feel—" he gasps, his hips stuttering as he drops back down. "Why is it always so good?"

I wish I knew. It's rare that he's vocal, but when he is, he's usually singing me little praises. Thanking me for the good dick or telling me how hot I am. I've never been praised, never had anyone so lost in the pleasure that I give them that they can't help but be grateful for it. It's a heady thing, being able to make this specific boy enjoy me so much.

He has to lean back so he can brace himself on the mattress, riding me faster until his breathing picks up in pitch.

"I'm close," I warn him, reaching out to stroke the dick bouncing in time with his hips to hopefully bring him over the edge with me. He sits down, pins me with all his weight so he can roll his body over mine, and thrust his cock through my fist.

"Come on," he demands, getting desperate the closer he gets.

He's a big guy, but I'm able to lift him, roll him under me so that I can finish us off. He's too distracted to react—simply wraps his legs around me and tells me to fuck him, to fill him up. That sizzling heat is spreading, climbing up my spine and urging me to move faster, harder. I can feel his fingers digging into my back, grating over my shoulder blades with every thrust I give him.

It's a struggle to grip his cock between us, but I'm too close. I need him to come first, stroke him with a goal in mind, and immediately breathe out in relief when cum finally spills from his tip. My dick twitches in sync with his, and it feels like my heart starts to beat slower as my entire world zeroes in on us. It's just me and Cade, our pleasure and pains. His arms are still wrapped around me, his fingertips now just gently trailing soft touches along the scratches he's etched into my back. It feels like I could fall asleep like this, using his shoulder as my pillow.

"Nic?"

I'm still inside him, can feel myself throbbing as I push up enough to look at him. This time he doesn't ask, just leans up and presses his lips against mine. It's sweet and innocent—so unlike everything else we do. It's hard to think as he does it, but it's over quickly. Like he knows I'm nervous about it.

I've kissed, been kissed. I'm just not good at it. It's only happened once, and I know it's a stupid reason to hold back, but embarrassing myself in front of Cade isn't something I handle very well. And I'm so good at making him come that having him tell me my kisses suck would have been... I'm grateful that he's kept it innocent.

"Leg still hurt?"

I huff a laugh against his face and go back to laying

on his shoulder. "No." It does a little, but that's okay.

"Orgasms as pain management. McDreamy knew what he was talking about. Though, I don't remember if that guy actually jerked off or if he just watched porn, but—"

"What the fuck are you talking about?"

"Grey's Anatomy."

"What?"

"It's a show. You've never seen it?"

I snort, burying my face deeper into his neck so he can feel me shake my head. Obviously, I've heard of it. I'm sure I've seen parts of episodes and clips, but why is this being discussed right now of all times? He's so random.

"No way. We gotta remedy that shit right now. Move." He taps my ribs, but I don't budge. "Let me get my iPad."

"No." I stay right where I am, breathing him in as the cum on his abs works to glue us together. It's too comfortable. Makes me wish we'd been sleeping —actually sleeping—together this whole time. Makes me wish we could do it forever.

Twenty

Nic

My last good Christmas involved homemade reindeer food and traps for elves that I knew didn't exist. I was too old for the kinds of shit my mom liked doing, but it made her happy. The Christmas after that, I was forced to spend time with my dad and his new family—my first holiday with Tracey and Cade.

Seeing my dad happy had the exact opposite effect that seeing my mom happy did. It made me sick—physically ill. I didn't understand why my mom was suffering while he was living life exactly the same as always—the only difference was that it wasn't with us. He had a new wife, one who wasn't prone to major depressive episodes, and a son who didn't resent him. It felt like an injustice.

I can hear Cade downstairs in the kitchen. I don't know what he's doing, but all the noise is stressing me out. I don't want him to try and make today special. I don't want to have to hurt his feelings when I end up not being able to muster up any fake smiles.

Things are different between us. Sex and isolation will do that, but I can see through it—the bullshit. I know that things have an expiration date. Riding my dick doesn't change that. Playing doctor with my fucked up legs definitely doesn't change it, but I don't know if he realizes that. He keeps touching me in ways that feel so... loving. Maybe. I don't know if anyone has every touched me lovingly, so maybe I'm wrong.

I probably am wrong. There's this constant undercurrent of dread threatening me no matter how good things feel with Cade. We can be binging his favorite shows, laughing and touching, and it means nothing. Not when I know that it'll end. It'll end up being like all the good times with my mom—nothing but memories.

I kind of want to leave. We came in my car, so it's not like I don't have the option. I don't know what I would do or where I would go, but at least I wouldn't be so antsy. I could go see my mom—I *should* go see my mom. I was going to in a week anyway.

But I don't want to get up.

"Nic?"

I open my eyes but can't seem to bring myself to do anything more. I listen to the sounds of him walking further into the room and still can't be bothered to turn around. It seems like too much work to roll over and look at him. And I'm not sure I could handle it if I did. I'm a bundle of nerves and don't even know why. My heart is trying to hammer itself into an upset, beating faster for no reason.

"Are you hungry?"

He doesn't give me the chance to ignore him, climbs in bed with me, and hooks a leg over my hip so that I have no choice but to acknowledge him. I can feel his breath on the back of my neck just as his hand slips under my shirt, his fingers warm as they fan out over my abs.

"I'm good." I can't help but lean back and press my body into his. It helps, having him all over me like this. It's calming—like my own living, breathing Xanax. With his body heat keeping me warm, I don't have to wonder if he wants me here or if he's sad that he's stuck with me on today of all days. It allows me to take a deep breath, almost a sigh of relief.

How pathetic.

He doesn't know how to deal with me like this. We've gotten cozy together. We share a room and have the same job, and for the past few days, we've spent every single hour together. I can feel myself shutting down, sinking into the beginnings of misery, and he's noticing. He's tried to get me up a few times to no avail. He doesn't know that it's just the day—my mom and the fact that once again my dad doesn't want me here—and he wouldn't understand. It's like the less I respond, the touchier he gets.

His fingertips slip under the band of my sweats, his palm smoothing over my happy trail as his hand slides lower. I expect him to do more, go for my dick like a normal person, but he just keeps gently caressing my groin.

"What the hell are you doing?"

He snickers behind me, pulling his hand out of my pants and rolling over me with a grunt. "What, I can't cop a feel?"

"Of my pubes?" I cock a brow at him, matching the little half-assed grin he gives me.

"They're soft." He shrugs. "Let's do something."

I sigh. "I *was* doing something."

"Yeah, as cool as sleeping the day away is, I think we should do something else. Like, hmm, get up?"

I want to protest, tell him that I hate Christmas and I don't want to celebrate. But he is stuck with me, and I feel a little guilty for it. Maybe even more than a little.

"What do you want to do?"

His smile grows, deepening that cute little divot in his chin. It's on impulse that I touch him, plant my thumb right there over the scruff he hasn't shaved once since we got here. I didn't realize he even had to shave so much, but he must. I'm pretty sure he shaves more than I do. Asshole grows hair better than I do. No surprise there.

"We can hang in the treehouse?"

I don't know what I expected, but it definitely wasn't that.

"We can bring a bunch of blankets and my iPad and watch movies. Or more Grey's."

I let my thumb slide across his lips, feeling my chest tighten as he waits for my answer. It feels like he deliberately chose something not at all Christmas-like for me.

"Hm, I would—" I purse my lips, teasing him as I

remember something from forever ago. "But I'm not allowed in the treehouse."

He rolls his eyes, but to be fair, it's true. He banned me himself years ago. At one point, there was even a poorly drawn sign stating so—before his mom made him take it down. But I didn't want to go in there anyway. It was designated for Liam and Cade, and I wanted no part of that.

I think I was jealous. I didn't have friends, and seeing those two together all the time reminded me of that. Also, my dad built that treehouse for Cade. He never built one for me.

But it sounds okay now. Being alone with Cade in tight spaces—that's pretty much the only thing I like doing these days.

"I'm officially unbanning you, Nic. Congrats." He climbs back over me, almost kneeing me in my ribcage instead of just getting off on his side of the bed. And I have no choice but to get up when he pulls my comforter away. "Let's go."

We wrangle up as many blankets as we can and head out there. It's colder than I expected, but Cade's suggestion that we use each other for warmth seems like a good enough idea to me. Plus, we've found almost every blanket in the house to pile up into a nest. Once I'm sinking into it, I can definitely see myself sweating up here eventually. Especially with as touchy as Cade can be.

It becomes clear that it was a planned event when he pulls out a tumbler of hot chocolate. And when he skips over all the Christmas shit Netflix has and starts suggesting scary movies, I know that it's definitely for me. He's aware the day has me down and is actively trying to keep my mind off of it.

I don't know what to make of it, but as the movie we pick starts, I know that I'm grateful that he forced me out here—and not just to the treehouse. If I'd stayed at the apartment alone, I know I'd be in bed doing nothing but letting myself feel bad.

It's not a fair trade—I get him coddling me and doing what he can to make sure I'm not sad, and he gets... nothing. Me. It's not a fair trade at all, but I'm letting myself be a little selfish.

The only reminder I get of what day it is is a short *Merry Christmas* text from Baby, but I don't even open it. I do check to see if my dad sent anything, but I figure it's best to just turn my phone off when I find nothing. Before I can be too bothered by it, Cade's wrapping an arm around me and spewing nonsense about how he would have for sure been too smart to fall for the killer's bullshit as he once again makes me the little spoon.

"Why am I always the little spoon?"

"Because I realized you're shorter than me."

"By an in—" I shut my mouth when he starts to laugh.

"I'm just the big spoon, emo boy. I don't know what else to tell you. If you don't like it, I can—"

I push him back to where he is when he tries to crawl over me. "I didn't say that."

He places a kiss behind my ear as he burrows into me, throwing his leg over mine. "I got you something."

"Why?" I sit up, forcing him off of me as I move to face him. It's a stupid question, but for a moment, I'm genuinely confused. He's never given me anything, not ever. We're not those kinds of brothers—at least, we didn't used to be. And I know that gifts are a normal part of this stupid fucking day, but I thought we'd settled on pretending it was just any other boring day—that's what I was banking on.

We had a few gifts from our parents under their tree that we opened a couple days ago because we —Cade—didn't want to didn't want to wait. It really pointed out just how little they know me. Cade got clothes that I know he'll wear, the Oculus headset that he's been talking about for a while, and some other random things I know he was happy to open. I got a couple band tees from bands I don't listen to, some school supplies for the upcoming semester and gifts cards. I think he felt sorry for me, watching me open them and knowing me enough to know that they weren't gifts that were purchased with me in mind.

So maybe that's why he got me something— because he feels sorry for me. I think that's why he does half the things he does for me. Pity.

"I don't know." He digs under our pile of blankets and pulls out a small black box. "I know we aren't celebrating, but it *is* Christmas, and I just..." He shrugs, looking at my chest as a faint blush spreads over his cheeks. "I wanted to, I guess."

"Cade," I start, holding back the annoyance I shouldn't be feeling. But I thought that we had an unspoken deal. "I didn't get you anything." I'm kind of mad that I didn't.

"That's fine. I didn't expect you to."

He doesn't even say it like it upsets him, and that makes it so much worse. Truthfully, I did think about it, getting him a gift, but I didn't think we were the kinds of people who got each other presents. I've known him for nearly half my life and have never given him a single thing. Not unless bruises and hard-ons count.

When I make no moves to reach for it, he opens it for me. It's a necklace. Nothing fancy. A small silver chain with a solid black dog tag hanging off it.

"I don't wear necklaces." I'm being a dick, I know that. I can tell he's nervous giving it to me, but I don't understand why he'd do this.

"I know. It's—you don't need to wear it. It's more..." He stops talking. Picks it up and opens the necklace. It's a locket, and I'm even more confused now. "It's you and your mom. Just to have."

"What?" I take it out of his hand and hold it in the minimal light slipping through the sheet we have covering the door. I inspect it up close and see a small black-and-grey image engraved into the metal. It's me and my mom sporting big, toothy smiles. It's one of the pictures I have of her in my photo album. I keep it in the bedside table between our beds—meaning he must have gone through my things to get it. Maybe I should be mad, but I'm not. It's a good gift.

It was before she got sad. Or sadder, I guess. Before my adult teeth came in, and the vitiligo was only just starting to spread more.

"There's two." He pulls another box out of his pocket and opens that one too. "I figured your mom would like one," he stuns me by saying. "You can give it to her the next time you see her or whenever." Another shy little shrug, and it hits me right then that he doesn't know.

"Oh."

"Here." He sets the packaging in my hands and moves to turn back around. "We should probably go inside. It's getting dark, and—"

"Cade." I grab his wrist to stop him from leaving our cozy little nest. "Thank you." My throat feels thick and is burning with the urge to cry. He got my mom a Christmas present—thought of her when nobody else does anymore. Not my dad. Not even Paulina. It's been up to me alone to remember her. "She... thank you."

I think my mom would like Cade. Maybe. If she could get past him being the other woman's son. And she'd love the necklace. It's not expensive, not even something a woman would wear, but it's sweet and thoughtful and she'd love it.

"You're welcome." He smiles, genuinely happy that I'm grateful for the gifts. "I figured you guys missed each other, so..."

My chest swells with so much adoration, so much gratitude and love that it's almost overwhelming. I don't know what to do with all of it. I was blaming missing my mom for my bad mood, but it's more than that. It's Cade. It's the timer we have on this thing. I just don't want it to end.

"Thanks." I lean forward and kiss him, a small peck before I pull away awkwardly and laugh through my nose when his eager lips follow mine.

He reads me so well it'd be creepy if I wasn't so obsessed with him. Like knowing I don't want to celebrate Christmas or that I'm missing my mom. Knowing that despite spitting in his mouth, I don't want his tongue in mine. He just pays attention to things, to me, and it blows my mind. I don't deserve it.

I let him keep kissing me, reveling in the added weight when he settles over my lap. Listen to his blissful little moans as he grinds his hips into mine. His lips start to move down, his stubble scratching against mine as he nips over my jaw, moving lower and lower. I have to tug on his hair to stop him from sucking on my neck, and am so fucking happy hearing the sound of his laugh.

"Cade," I murmur, closing my eyes when he gives me his undivided attention. I love him. I am in love with him, want shit that just isn't possible, and I don't know what to do. So, I ask him the stupidest question I've ever asked anyone. "What are we?"

"You—" The question stumps him, and with every split second he goes not giving me an answer I want to hide that much more. "I... don't know."

My head nods despite the disappointment I feel, my body fully accepting his nonanswer. It makes sense. I'm not sure either, so I don't know why I expected anything more from him.

"Nic."

I can't stand it. "It's fine."

"I don't—"

"Cade, it's fine." I open my eyes to give him a wan smile—try to make it less sad, but know that I fail.

"Stop. That's not—"

"It's fine," I say again, grab a hold of his hips so that I can push him off of me, but he panics.

"Wait!" He holds my face between his hands, distressed that I might pull away. "Nic, I'm not saying —of course, I want—fuck. *Fuck*, Nic." His forehead rests against mine, and I just sit there. Wait. Hope that he doesn't disappoint me anymore, but finding it unbelievable that he won't. "What about my mom? Your dad?"

It's a good point. One I've wondered about myself is when I let myself wish for more. "I get it," I tell him truthfully. I do. He has so much more to lose than me. People to disappoint. Picking me over anything else isn't some easy choice for him. It's not even a plausible one.

It was a silly lapse in judgment. I knew what my role was in this situation, but the necklaces had me losing brain cells. I won't let it happen again.

"Nic, do you—are you saying you'd date me? Be my boyfriend?"

I take a second to examine his face, try to make sense of what it is he wants me to say here, and come up short. My open book is very hard to read at the moment. I want to say yes. The word boyfriend never crossed my mind, but Cade is mine. He feels like mine, and anything else doesn't make sense. Nothing else feels right. But I play it safe.

"No. No, that's not what I meant. I just wanted to know what we were doing."

"Oh." He relaxes on top of me, his entire body slumping in relief as he looks down, probably hiding the look that says he dodged a bullet. "Well... I don't see why anything has to change, right?" His fingers flex where they've moved to the tops of my shoulders, and at least I know where he stands on that.

"I guess."

"It's just... they're getting married soon, you know?"

"What?" I have no clue what he's talking about. It takes me a second to assume that he means Tracey and Anton. They're already married, but I know she's been asking for an actual wedding for a long time.

"Their wedding? They—did your dad not tell you?"

The look on my face tells him that I have zero clue what he's talking about.

"Oh." He's uncomfortable. Even he knows that my dad should have told his own fucking son that he was having a wedding soon—especially since it's so close to my mom's death date. "Well, yeah. They are."

Nobody thought to fucking tell me—not even Cade? Am I even invited?

"Your dad and my mom never had a wedding and decided that now was a good time. My mom has wanted one for a while. Years, y'know? And I don't want to ruin things for her. I'm supposed to walk her down the aisle, and she doesn't need to be thinking about you and me fucking while that happens."

You and me fucking. It's hard to believe that it's all it

is, that there isn't more between us, but that was just me being fucking stupid.

"You're walking her down the aisle?"

"Yeah." He smiles, and I feel that little grin like a punch to my chest. This is a fun thing for him. Something special he gets to share with his mom. With my dad. He's a part of it while I'm...

I don't even want to be a part of it. My mom doesn't deserve that. If my mom were getting married, I'd love to walk her down the aisle, so I don't blame Cade for being happy for his mom.

I doubt I'll even go, that they even want me there. I know Tracey doesn't. And Cade, how would he act around me if I did go? They both think he hates me —what if he thinks he needs to keep that up? I'm not going, not dealing with that.

"When is it?"

His answer solidifies the choice for me. I have plans that day anyway.

Twenty-One

Cade

"It's not too late, y'know?" I run my thumb over one of his scars, caressing him under the blankets as he lies lifeless in front of me. I don't want to leave him today, but I have to. It's my mom's wedding, of course I have to. But he's been... I'm not a doctor, so I can't be sure, but I genuinely think he's depressed. He has a history of it, but I've never seen him like this. He's usually mad. Quiet and broody but pissed off. This is not that.

But it could be the wedding—the one he's refusing to go to. He's never been okay with their relationship. My pigheadedness kept me from sympathizing with him, but I understand it more now. His parents were happily married at one point, and now only one of them is.

So, I'm hoping it's just the wedding. I don't know what else it could be.

"I don't want to go."

I knew he would say that, but I'm still

disappointed. I hug him tighter, pulling him back until I'm touching him as much as possible. "Nic." I kiss his shoulder, right on one of the many tiny pale circles of skin I adore.

"I don't want to—"

"I know you don't want to go. But what are you going to do for two days without me?" It's a poorly attempted joke, but really, I need to know. He hasn't been doing well, and I don't know what to do about it. I want to help him, but I don't know how. If I'm not here, who will make sure he eats? Gets out of bed? What if he hurts himself?

I don't think he will—I don't *want* to think he will, but he has before.

My arm tightens around him and squeezes until he grunts. He never answers me, and it stresses me out more than it should. Or maybe I'm not stressed enough. I'm not sure—I have plans to ask his dad about this. They're not close, but he took Nic's mental health seriously when he lived with us, so maybe he'll have a better idea of how to navigate things.

"Nic, I—"

"Cherry."

I freeze. It's not until he's jerking the arm I have trapped under mine that I pull back, being slow with it because I have no clue how to take this.

"Get off of me. Leave, Cade."

"Nic." I don't mean to sound so hurt, but why is he doing this—what did I do?

"It works both ways—it means stop. Leave me alone."

"I—okay." I stare for a while at his shoulder, at that spot I just kissed. My body is reacting to that little word like it's an omen, a terrible sign, and I'm not at all prepared for it. I don't want to leave him. My hand reaches for him, a last-ditch effort to reason with him, but he pulls away and scoots closer to the wall and away from me. "Okay," I whisper, going against my instincts because it's what he wants. If it were me who said it—though I know I never would—he'd immediately stop all movement. He'd respect my wishes.

So I get up, grab the overnight bag I have packed, and step out of the room. I can't look at him before I go because I might end up back in bed with him to try to get him to talk to me.

Every step I take that means he gets further away breaks a little piece of me. Cherry. I knew when he gave that to me that I'd hate it, but I never expected this. This pain. Cherry.

Baby isn't in his room when I check, and right as I'm about to text him to ask where he is, he comes out of the bathroom.

"I thought you had a wedding to go to." He fixes his tiny pair of pink shorts, the only thing he's wearing, like he's trying to protect the modesty that definitely doesn't exist when he's dressed like that.

"It's tomorrow." I clear my throat to try and rid my voice of the misery I feel. "I'm going home tonight, but I wanted to ask if you could do me a favor."

"Maybe."

"It's..." I'm not sure if it's a good idea to ask him

to look after Nic and check on him a few times while I'm away, but it's definitely a bad idea to do nothing. I try to think of a way to word it so that I don't share too much—it's not my place to tell Baby Nic has issues. "Nic isn't feeling well."

"Because he wasn't invited to your parents' wedding?" He looks genuinely sympathetic before he walks to his room, giving me a view of his ass peeking out from the bottom of his shorts. I'd remind him about his own no-nudity rule if his question didn't surprise me.

"He was invited. He's just… sick."

"Oh." He climbs on his bed, hugging one of his stuffed animals to his bare torso. "What's wrong with him?"

"I don't—he has chronic pain." It's not a lie and more believable than a cold.

"Oh, he should have told me. I have some gummies that—"

"No, that's fine. I just wanted you to check on him and make sure he was doing okay while I was gone. Please?"

He has a tiny smile on his lips as he nods his head. "Yeah, I can do that."

"What?"

"What do you mean?"

"Why are you looking at me like that?" It's making me self-conscious and maybe a little paranoid. I told Nic I was fine telling people about us—as long as we held off on our parents for a while—but he didn't want that. I wanted it. I said it like I didn't care either way, but I want to be able to say that I have someone. That I'm not alone, and more than that, that I have *Nic*. I'd love to show him off or be someone he'd be happy to do the same with, but he said that he preferred keeping things as they were. It bothers me, and it's one of the many other things that make me self-conscious, but I don't want to upset him.

And I can deal. As long as I still get to have him, it's okay.

But things don't feel as good as they were. I'm not even sure I do have him. The new doubt is worse than any of the bullshit I was wallowing in before we started whatever this whole thing is. I don't want to lose him.

"I don't know. You're just cute when you're in love with someone other than Liam."

"Wha—"

His smile grows, and I decide it's best to save face. "Shut up." I shut his door as I leave, cutting off his quiet laugh.

I'm not in love with Nic. Not... I don't think I'm in love with Nic. It wasn't like this with Liam. That was unrequited, but I was sure I was in love with him. This is different.

It's more like an obsession. And sometimes, it feels so... unruly. It feels like my whole existence begins and ends with him. He's every bit of havoc and harmony in my own little world, bigger than anything else I've ever dealt with. I loved Liam, and even though I can't love him how I once wanted to, I know that he'll always be a part of my life. Things with Nic are more fragile, like an antique vase sitting too close to the edge of the shelf. One good jolt and it'll shatter, and most of the time, shit with Nic is a little bumpy.

Loving Liam was scary, but whatever this is with Nic is fucking terrifying.

That word, the safeword he gave me, plays on a loop as I leave the apartment. It's eating at me. Leaving him alone—it feels dangerous. He's probably just going to go back to sleep, and Baby did say he'd check on him, but I feel so aimless the more distance I put between us.

I have to borrow a tie from Liam. I'd originally asked him if I could take two because I'd hoped Nic would change his mind, but that didn't work out. Nic turned down more than just an invite—that only came after he said he didn't want to be in the wedding. I wish his dad had asked him sooner and given him more time to prepare. I wasn't aware that he hadn't even bothered to tell him there was going to be a wedding at all, but asking if he'd stand up there by the altar just days before it was supposed to happen seemed like an afterthought. I'm sure that's how it felt to Nic.

He doesn't say it, but I know it hurts him that Anton doesn't try harder with him. Nic tries to act like he doesn't care, but he slips all the time and shows me bits and pieces of things just beneath all the cracks. I just wish that Nic didn't push him away so much.

Seeing Jax sitting in front of Liam's apartment door again most likely means that I'll have to wait longer than I was expecting for him to answer the door, so I send Liam a text and hope it speeds things along.

"Hey." I sit next to him on the welcome mat.

Jax chooses to flip me off instead of a greeting, but the bruise on his chin tells me that it's probably only so he can hide his face.

"What's this?" I barely brush his jaw before he's flinching away. "You okay?"

"I'd be a lot better if your bestie wasn't the actual horniest bottom to exist. What does he even eat? Because I really don't understand how a dude's ass can be so ready for dick at every hour of the fucking day."

I laugh, letting him get away with the deflection. It's none of my business.

"You sound jealous."

"Fuck off. I'm not jealous. I'm... well, you know what, maybe I am. My ass hurts from sitting on this stupid cold floor waiting for Princess Liam to be done with my best friend—and! By the time that happens, *his* ass is gonna be hurting in an entirely different way, and yeah. I'm a little jealous of that, but not because I want Seb's stupid dick. Or Liam's!"

"Okay."

"I just want some idiot to tell me they'd build me a pond if I ever turned into a duck, y'know? Why is that so hard to find?"

"I—" Have no clue what he's talking about. "I'm not sure, Jax."

"Whatever. And what about you—do you bottom? Does your ass hurt?"

I shrug with a smirk. "A little bit, actually." No

point denying it, not to Jax. He knows more than anyone how wrapped up I am in Nic.

"Ugh. Well, unless you're willing to share him, I—"

"Nope. He likes his ass a little less yappy."

He frowns at me, a look so genuinely solemn for a moment that it has me going quiet—it reminds me of how I'm feeling. "They all do!" He leans his head on my shoulder and sniffles, and I can't tell if he's being serious or not. "I'm going to be single for... til the end of fucking time apparently because nobody likes hot as fuck twunks who maybe have a hard time shutting up sometimes. Which—" He sits up, getting fired up all over again and descending into a babbling madness. "Makes no sense if you think about it!" He leans back against the door with a thud, not even looking at me as he goes on. "Like... usually you'd want a mouth to be open, right? Can't stick your—*oh!*" He falls back, catching himself before he hits Liam's legs.

"What's—" Liam looks between us as I stand up, and I can see it when he decides that it's not worth it to ask. "I'll grab your tie."

"Thanks."

∞ ∞ ∞

"There's my boy!" My mom throws her arm around me, holding on for long enough that I breathe in a deadly dose of her perfume. "Come in, come in! Dinner is almost ready."

I'm still kind of mad at her, but I let her tug me inside anyway. Nic isn't here, and while yeah, he's a spiteful little shit who didn't even want to be here, I find it hard not to blame my mom. And Anton. They could have tried harder to include him in the process, asked him to come, and made it seem like they actually wanted him to. He's their kid—stepson to my mom, but a son nonetheless—and they don't even care if he's here or not. He's an adult, I get that, but the things they do have made him feel like he's not welcome, and it bothers me.

I realize I'm a piece of shit—that's nothing new —because I used to act the same way, only worse. But I've matured and so has Nic. I understand him a little more, see through the anger and contempt and see that really he's just lonely. He feels rejected, and everyone who should be there for him isn't.

It could be a symptom—the Dumb Dick is still going strong—but I feel it all on his behalf regardless.

Plus, the fucking affair nobody bothered to tell me about. It's fully impossible not to be upset about that. I thought I knew my mom pretty well, but I guss not.

I'm at least happy that Anton is more disappointed that Nic isn't here than I expected.

"I wish he'd changed his mind. Did he say why he didn't want to come?"

It's sort of stupid that he'd even ask that question. How he doesn't realize that is beyond me. It's never been a secret that Nic doesn't approve of this blended family of ours.

"He just didn't want to."

I hear his voice and that word again, feel like a thorn in my chest. He wanted me to leave him. That's why he said it, right?

"Well, as much I wish he could just be happy for us, I have to say that I'm glad he didn't bring his negativity here." My mom scoops some of her salad in her mouth, and I know it's not entirely unreasonable of her to say, but it still bugs me. "This is a happy occasion."

"Honestly, he seems kind of sad." I purposefully ignore my mom's retort. Their wedding will be happy, but that has nothing to do with my worries for Nic.

She purses her lips in a tight line when I look at her, clearly unhappy with the topic being discussed. But my stepdad needs to know.

"What do you mean?" Anton sets his glass of wine down without taking a sip, his bushy brows pitched low in concern. I've only ever seen the one picture of Nic's mom, but from what I can tell, he's all her. I've never met Carrie, but I wonder if he gets any of his personality from her too. I suspect he gets some of the depression from her, at least.

"The past few days he just doesn't do much. Works or sleeps, and that's it. He wasn't like that before." He sits in bed most of the time, regardless of how happy or sad he is, but his mood is noticeably different. And he stopped working out completely. He's just different. It was headed this way before our Christmas break, but things sort of plummeted when we got back.

"Is he taking his meds?"

"I—what meds?" I look at my mom, see her quietly watching us, and think for the first time that I maybe should have waited until I could speak to Anton privately before bringing things up. If Nic didn't want me to know about it, he certainly wouldn't want her to know. Unless he really isn't taking them. I've seen a prescription topical steroid cream and ibuprofen, but that's it.

But then I remember what he said while he was drunk—how his meds didn't react well with ibuprofen and alcohol. He claimed it caused his nosebleed, but that was the only nosebleed I saw him get—does that mean he did stop taking things?

How could I forget something that important? I wanted to do some snooping to find out what he was on, but it never came up again. I should have paid better attention.

It feels like I'm fucking things up. He deserves better, and it's killing me that I can't give him that. I don't know how.

"I'll call him."

That won't do any good. I highly doubt Nic would answer a phone call from him—especially with the wedding being tomorrow. But he can do what he wants. "What do we do to make him less... is there anything I should watch out for?"

"You're not a babysitter, Cade. You're both adults, and you have school and work to worry about. Not your stepbrother."

"Trace." Anton looks at his wife in mild disappointment, mirroring how I feel.

"I'm just saying." She pats her husband's hand, trying to soften the blow of her dismissal. "It's not like Nic would do anything to help Cade if the roles were reversed."

I don't tell her that I think he might, but I really do. He cares about me, I know it. I feel it. "I just want to know what to look out for," I say, all my focus on Anton—on the one other person in the room who cares.

"I think as long as—"

"Tony, come on. He's just upset about the wedding —about his mother and all the crap he's always upset about. He's fine."

"His mother—what is today?" He reaches for his phone, his expressive brows raising when he spots what he's looking for. "Shit." He sighs heavily, wiping his hand over the short beard on his face.

"What?"

"It's the anniversary of her death tomorrow. I forgot." He looks at his wife, but she doesn't seem concerned in the slightest. This isn't news to her at all.

"Her *death*? What do you mean?" How could I not know that? Why would he not tell me? "Whe—how?"

"He didn't tell you?"

"No, he—how did she die?"

"She... killed herself. Nic was trying to get her into a treatment facility, but..."

That's horrible. It makes my blood run cold to have this bomb dropped on me like this. It makes me want to go to Nic, see him and check on him but I can't. I fucking can't because he said *cherry.*

No wonder he misses her so much—he hardly ever mentions her, but when he does, he speaks like it physically hurts him. The fucking necklaces I got— what an awful gift. And...

"You guys are throwing a party on the day Nic's mom died?"

"It's not a party," my mom scolds. "It's a wedding, and... there were only so many dates available." She gives the table a flippant shrug that has me stunned.

"Mom, you knew? That's—no shit, he didn't want to come." I sit back and stare at her as I process all the many bits and pieces of information being thrown at me. He was just lying in bed, right where he had been for the majority of the last three days, and I *left* him.

"Language."

"It's my fault," Anton butts in. "I should have remembered."

"But my mom did remember. Right?" I question her, genuinely hoping that she didn't. "You didn't really expect him to come, did you?"

Just watching her face I can tell that I'm right. They could have picked a different date. Taken more time to plan the wedding, maybe even have it on their actual anniversary so they don't end up with two, but she chose to marry Nic's dad on the day his mom died. It's not... no it is. It's fucked up. Nic deserves better, a stepmom who gives a fuck and has sympathy for him. A dad who sticks up for him.

A boyfriend who cares enough to be there for him when he needs him.

"You should reschedule."

"That's not an option."

"Mom, it's not even a real wedding—you're already married."

"Maybe we should, Trace."

My mom gapes at her husband, her cheeks flushing the longer she sits with his words. "No." She shakes her head, adding to the bit of finality in her tone. "No. I'm not doing that. I've been waiting for this for years. I'm not going to let him ruin it. I'm getting married, and my son is going to walk me down the aisle—I deserve that."

"But *my* son isn't even going to be there."

"Cade is your son too!"

"You know what I mean."

"Mom," I cut in because I need to know. "Did you purposefully schedule it on this day?"

Her eyes roll, and it's the only answer she gives me. It's the only one I need.

"Then... I'm not walking you down the aisle."

Twenty-Two

Nic

There's some dirt that needs clearing, a few rocks and weeds, but it doesn't take long. It's not much, but it makes me feel better just looking at it when I'm done. Seeing her name all crisp and clean on the headstone I picked out just over a year ago now.

It feels weird to talk to her. I don't know what I believe in as far as the afterlife goes, but I do feel her. Sometimes. Not as much as I wish I could, but then maybe that's a good thing. Maybe that means she's usually somewhere else, a place where she's happy. Somewhere I'm not.

I don't know that there's any amount of therapy that could ever convince me that my not being enough for her wasn't one of the reasons she left me. She never did get over losing her baby, and though I've lost count of how many times I've been told that I was enough, the evidence says otherwise.

And with my dad... I just don't get why neither of

my parents ever put me first. That's what parents are supposed to do. But I'm not here to dwell on all of that. I can do that anytime.

"There's not much to say." I shrug, picking at the grass in front of her headstone in a way that reminds me of Cade's fidgeting. "I'm doing good."

Most of the time.

"I... moved in with Cade—my stepbrother." I don't remember us ever talking about Tracey and Cade when she was alive. My dad's new family didn't feel like a safe topic. "But it's only temporary," I try to reassure her, just in case she's against the idea. "He's not so bad." I smile as I think about him, feeling bittersweet as I sit here talking to a dead woman about a boy who I have no future with, who she'll never even get to meet. "He—" I almost tell her that he left today, that he went to the wedding, but I know she doesn't want to hear about that. "I think you'd like him. He's... kind of annoying, but he makes me laugh."

There's no telling how long I can handle keeping things between us quiet. Loving him in private only to pretend he doesn't mean everything to me in public... that's not something I can do long-term.

But then, it was never going to be long-term anyway, and I knew that. I do have enough saved up, at least I think so. And even if he did end up telling his mom about us, what happens when she's against it? I don't think he'd pick me over her, not in any scenario.

"I think I need help, Mom," I say out loud because I honestly do. I just feel so... sad. It reminds me of her, and I hate that. I need to get back on my meds.

I haven't even ended things with Cade, and already, it feels like my heart is breaking. It feels like something I won't recover from.

I don't want to live like her. She was so sad all the time, and it was horrible. She just wasted away, and that will not be me, especially not because of a boy. I won't let it be.

But she was never anybody's first choice, and I'm not either. Sometimes, the weight of that is just too much. It feels like it holds me back.

"I love you, Mom." I don't know what else to say, so I figure I may as well leave it at that. I'm about to get up when I remember the necklace in my pocket. I pull it out and look at it, let it soothe a tiny piece of me. I'll have to make sure that I get her gifts from now on, that way, she keeps getting something—something other than the flowers I already bring. Because Cade won't be giving either of us anymore after this.

"This is a Christmas gift from Cade." I open the locket, wishing she could see the little image of me and her, both of us so happy, but knowing she can't. I don't feel her and haven't since I sat down. She left —another person who didn't care enough about me to prioritize me. But I still give her time to see it, just in case. The moon is bright, and if I hold it just right, I can see both of us smiling. I close it and pull a small patch of grass up, just big enough that the necklace will fit so that I can cover it back up. "Bye, Mom."

It's cold, making it a little difficult to force my stiff muscles to cooperate as I stand up, but I manage. I've only been here an hour, meaning it's not even one in the morning yet, and I did originally plan on staying longer.

But I'm still tired and just want to climb back into bed—probably Cade's bed—and sleep. I don't think it could hurt any more than it already will when things end between us, so I suppose the best thing to do is enjoy it while it lasts.

I don't expect to see him when I turn around, but there he is. The moonlight allows me to see him clearly, dressed snugly in a snug winter coat. Of course, he was smart enough to bring one, and I'm over here shivering like a moron. It has me grinning, genuinely happy to see him. It's such an intense contrast , such a relief after everything I was just feeling that it has my eyes tearing up.

I start walking towards him, needing him in a way that makes it impossible not to. I'm so grateful when he starts walking too, faster than I am so that we get to each other sooner.

"What are you—"

"I love you."

I freeze and stare at him in silence as an unshed tear finally slips free. "You love me?" It feels like a joke. Loving me is… it's too hard. If he loved me, why would he be against telling people about us? He tried to say that we could—as long as we kept it from his mom—but I could tell he didn't want to. He was just trying to make me feel better.

It doesn't make sense for him to love me.

"I do. You—I love you so fucking much, Nic." His forehead is warm against mine, his breath warming my cold lips.

"But you don't want anyone to know?" My voice is calm as I ask. But how does that make sense? He only wants to love me quietly, and how is that possible? Loving Cade quietly only works for me because my insides are constantly screaming with it—and I don't see that working for very long.

"No. I mean, yes, I do. We can tell everyone. Anton, my mom. Our roommates, Liam. We can tell whoever you want, Nic. We can be you and me together. Out loud."

Our parents... "What are you doing here? The wedding—"

"This felt more important. I just wanted to see you —tell you that I love you. That I want to be with you and that I don't care how mad my mom gets. I told them I was coming to find you."

He loves me. Maybe.

"How *did* you find me?" I go for the easiest question as a distraction, the rest of it too overwhelming to tackle just yet.

"I shared your location with me on your phone."

"I—you're such a stalker." And I don't even mind.

"I know. Can't help it." His lips brush against mine with barely enough contact to even be considered a kiss. "I love you."

I smile, finally wrapping my arms around him as I kiss him again.

"I love you, Cade."

∞ ∞ ∞

"Are you still cold?"

"I'm fine."

"Nic, don't—I hate when you say that."

I grin as my arms slip out of his jacket. "Sorry. But I really am. I'm good." He'd given me his coat to wear while we sat for a bit with my mom—while we talked about things I'd kept hidden from him. I know I need to get back on track with my mental health, and I'm glad he agrees. He didn't even talk about it like he thought I was a freak. He did call me stupid for using orgasms as a reason to stop my antidepressant, but I can't really say I regret it. We wouldn't be here right now if I hadn't done that.

"Do you have to leave in the morning?" I think about telling him that I'll go with him, but I just don't want to. My mom died a year ago, and I don't want to watch my dad marry her replacement on the same day. Cade has mentioned me holding grudges, and I wish I could help it, but I can't. It's difficult to let go of something that's bothered me for so long.

"No." He walks into me, his warm hands sliding under my shirt and around to rest on my back. "I had no idea that our parents... I get why you're so mad at them. I wish I'd known sooner. I don't really give a fuck about their wedding, and I don't want anything to do with it. Not when you're not going to be there." When his lips press against mine, I hold him there. Both of us linger, just savor the feel of each other's bodies pressed together. It's me who deepens the kiss. My mouth moves over his in sync, our lips wet as they glide across each other.

"Nic." He pulls back to look at me. "I don't know how it works—your..."

I try not to be bugged that he can't even say it, that he's treating it like a bad word, but it's hard. He's new to it. I've lived my life dipping in and out of depression. He has no idea, but he wants to. And I promised him back at my mom's grave that I would try harder to open up. Let him in. I need help, I know that. My mom was all alone, and I know I don't want to live like that. I worked hard after she passed to work on myself, and I let it all shatter as soon as I was getting somewhere.

"Cade," I murmur, moving my arms upwards so he can pull my shirt off. "Little brother," I tease, nipping at the corner of his smile as he undoes our jeans. "It's like you said—it's you and me. Us." *Out loud.* I feel warm and shivery as I say it, as I *feel* it. Not alone— what a crazy concept. "But first, I want you to fuck me."

He stops moving, leaning his head back a bit so that he can look at my face. I know that Cade is interested in topping me, so I'm not worried about any rejection.

"Are you sure?"

I nod my head, reaching into his pants to take him in hand. I'm not in a top kind of mood at the moment. I want to feel him inside me.

His breath tickles the skin on my shoulder as he moans at the touch. I walk him a few steps backward, but he stops when he hits the edge of my bed.

"I'm kind of nervous."

"You don't need to be," I tell him. "It's just us."

He makes no moves for the bed, so I move around him. He watches me lay down as he gets the lube, making sure to take his pants off before he moves onto the bed and then drags mine down my legs. I told him not to worry, but I am a little nervous too. It's not my first time, technically not even his, but it feels like it is. This doesn't feel like anything I've ever done before.

He's seen me naked, has even seen and touched my scars, but he's never seen me like this. Ready and waiting for him to work me open.

I don't have to ask him to go easy on me. The only experience he has with sex like this—with men —is what I've done to him—brutal fingers and hurried touches—but he reads me enough to know that I want something different.

It's uncomfortable at first—every finger he gives me elicits a burn that only goes away right before he adds another. It's been a while for me, and I know that it's going to hurt, but by the time he's got his cock lined up with my hole, I can't even think past the need to feel close to him.

"Wait," I hiss just as he pops through that second ring of muscle, breathing heavily as I try to bear down.

"More lube."

That has him laughing, slowly pulling out again so that he can do what I said. I have to grab my knees and bring them to my chest, trying to change the angle and make it easier when he fits the head back inside, stopping to give me time to adjust again. I nod my head after a moment, opening my eyes to check on him and finding him doing the same.

"Okay?"

I nod again, my tongue feeling too heavy to speak, and he gives me another inch, pausing when I blow out a slow breath so that he can grab my dick and stroke. The added sensation helps alleviate some of the pain, but not enough.

"Fuck, emo boy."

I huff a laugh, the sound getting cut off as he sinks in deeper. "Shit." I swear his dick has grown. He gives me a few slow, shallow thrusts before he's able to give me more, and I can tell he's holding back so much just by how tight his grip on my thigh is.

He slips over my prostate, finally giving me something that has me lighting up, and I blow out a breath in relief. "Right there," I moan, urging him to do it again with a soft push of my hips. "*Fuck.*" It's subtle, just a light stoking of the embers as he rocks his hips into mine, but it's perfect.

He falls into a steady rhythm, his breaths mingling with the sounds of my quiet moans. "Nic." He leans over me, his free hand sliding over my ribs and adding to all the pleasure flooding my senses. The hand working my dick starts to move faster, him hinting that he's close already by bringing me right there with him.

"I love you," he whispers against my mouth, and I can only nod my head again. "I could've sworn that I've been in love before, Nic, but I was wrong. This is— it's everything. *You're* everything." His eyelids flutter, struggling not to close the closer to the finish line he gets. "I don't think I could ever love you any more than I do right now."

My hand curls in the hair on the back of his head, tightening as he pegs that spot over and over, timing it perfectly with every tug on my cock.

I love him. Cade, my stepbrother. It almost feels like it happened too fast, but I think I've had feelings for him for a long time. He drives me crazy, can piss me off in ways that nobody else has ever managed, and I'm so fucking happy that he's mine—that he wants me as his.

My body locks up as I start to come, everything hitting me all at once. He keeps stroking me through it, only letting himself fall over the peak when the last pearl of cum falls onto my stomach.

"You okay?" He's breathing too heavily to be talking, but he's checking in on me, and I adore him for it. I don't take it anywhere near as easy on him when the roles are reversed—not until the very end— so I appreciate him giving me this gentleness.

"Mhm." But I lightly push at his abdomen, wanting him out of me.

"You know what I want to do?"

"Hm?"

"Get married."

"What?" I try to sit up, but he stops me with a hand on my chest. "Like... eventually?"

"No. I mean now. Like right now."

"Cade." I roll my eyes.

"I'm serious."

"We can't do that." I'm risking looking like an idiot by actually taking him seriously, but he seems so sincere, and I know that some people get crazy after sex.

"We can, though. We should."

"Are you—our parents are getting married today, Cade. You're fucking crazy."

"If I am, it's your fault. I think we should—maybe not today. But soon. Maybe tomorrow. I meant what I said: I can't imagine loving you anymore than I do right now. I want to feel like this forever. Will you marry me?"

Epilogue

Cade

Four days later...

"Get the fuck up! I'm not playing anymore, Cade. Checkout was fifteen minutes ago. We need to go!"

I flip him off, earning me a hard smack on my ass that has me yelping. "God—" I push my face into the hotel pillow to stop from complaining too loudly. "Is that any way to treat your husband?" My voice is wrecked, and I don't know if it's from all of the face fucking, the alcohol, or lack of sleep. Probably a combination of all three.

"You'll be my ex-husband if you don't get dressed." His voice moves farther away as he pretends he's responsible and rushes to gather our things. "And answer your fucking phone—it's been going off for the past hour."

I sit up enough to reach for the device, see Liam's name on my screen, and then immediately decline the call. I know what he wants. We waited a few days to actually tie the knot, feeling a little wary of the impulsivity of it all—*one* of us anyway—but once I convinced him, we drove here. Sin City, because where else were a couple of college kids going to get married? It was either here or BYU, and this place was closer.

We even got married before our parents, something I'm kind of tickled about. I mean, they've been married for years, but we at least beat them down the aisle. Anton put his foot down when he realized my mom's petty intentions. I don't know that they'll even have a wedding at all, and my mom is not taking it well. She's also not taking the news of our relationship well. All Anton did when he found out was send a simple congrats back in the group chat I created, but I had to temporarily block her after a few angry messages.

He did send me a private message that he wants to talk—which is understandable. I did marry his son out of nowhere. Not sure I wanna be doing that anytime soon, though.

And Liam is probably freaking out. It's not every day that your best friend marries their asshole stepbrother in a chapel where you can pick between Elvis, Dolly Parton, and Freddy Mercury to officiate.

I got a little drunk after we said I do, and I definitely sent some crazy pictures to... everyone: my mom, Liam, Baby, and probably Logan. I think I even emailed my freshman-year English professor. The only reason Nic is all disgusting and awake at the moment is because he held off on the booze—they don't mix well with the meds we picked up before leaving. I feel the tiniest bit bad that I made my brand spankin' new hubby watch after my obnoxious ass.

No ragrets, though.

Epilogue

Nic

Four years later...

"Does it matter?" I kiss the hollow of his throat just as I get his tie loosened enough to do so. "Whatever venue they pick, it won't be as cool as our wedding was."

He smiles, looking at me like he's every bit in love with me as he was four years ago. "That's true. I doubt they'll be able to swing Dolly Parton photobombing their kiss with her big ol' fake titties."

"See, it's gonna be boring."

"Yeah." He leans in to place a kiss on my lips. "You're still going."

I huff, finally finishing off the last button of his shirt.

"Don't pout. It makes me want to—"

"You know we can hear everything you guys are saying, right?" Liam says from just behind the changing room curtain. "And my wedding could kick your janky ass Vegas wedding's ass, okay?" He flings the curtain aside, leaving my shirtless husband standing there in front of the salesman, Sebastian, and Jax.

"Your nips are very pink, Cade," the yapper yaps.

"Didn't we leave him at Wetzel's Pretzels?" I swear most of the animosity is just because it's a habit by now, but mostly, he's very annoying—has been for four fucking years.

"You—"

"Jax." Cade grabs his T-shirt and puts it back on. "Come on. You promised you'd behave."

"What? He literally started it! You were standing right there."

I pick up the items we definitely won't be buying while they argue about it, and Liam ends up joining in on their fun. "Do you ever feel like you're actually an old man when you hang out with all of them?" Seb being an old man has been a running joke in the group ever since he hit thirty earlier in the year, but I really do think standing next to Jax—and yeah, sometimes my husband—makes anyone seem wise beyond their years.

"I feel like that every minute of every day." Sebastian leans forward to help me pick up some of the things Jax left in the booth just as one of the other sales associates tells the trio behind us to be quiet. "You're *in* the wedding, by the way. You have to come to the ceremony at least."

"Huh?"

"You're one of my groomsmen, Nic."

"I—Seb, is this you *asking* me to be one of your

groomsmen?"

"It wasn't really a question, but okay."

I snort. "Well, shit. Thanks for letting me know."

He nods his head, accepting my gratitude for what it is.

It sort of reminds me of my dad's wedding, of him asking if I'd stand in as his best man just three days before it was supposed to happen—the one that never did happen.

At least Sebastian gave me a few weeks.

I have to call him soon, my dad. Or not. I can wait until he calls me, and with my birthday coming up, I can assume that will be the day. As long as he doesn't forget.

Tracey keeps him busy, but ever since her attempt to try and steal my mom's death date, my dad does his best to keep her from being too... too much of a fuck nut, I guess. She still doesn't like me, though. But if she wants Cade around, she has no choice but to pretend she does.

He's not one to put up with any shit when it comes to me.

∞ ∞ ∞

"What are you working on?" I wrap my arms around his torso, resting my chin on his shoulder so that I can see the spread of papers that's keeping him from joining me in bed.

"It's... a romantic comedy. A gay romantic comedy, actually."

"Hm." I knew that because he's brought this very same project home everyday for the past two weeks. "Well, I think..." I grab the folder in his hand and slowly set it on the counter. "That all of this will still be here tomorrow."

"Nic—"

"And the deadline isn't even for another four weeks—you told me that. You have an entire marketing team working on this, right? You know as well as I do that by the time you decide on a spread, they're going to give you new material." I undo the button on his slacks, reaching in until I'm palming his cock in my hand.

"That happens sometimes, but—"

"You're coming to bed." I apply pressure, smiling when he leans into the touch with an airy sigh.

"That's—ugh. Fine." He leans his head back over my shoulder as I run my hand down his length. "You're lucky I'm horny."

"I know, my greedy boy. Come on."

"Did you hear Liam talking about adoption

yesterday? Can you imagine Sebastian as someone's dad? That'd be crazy."

"I think he'd be a good dad. Liam too."

"Hm. I guess. We wouldn't, though."

"No." I laugh behind him as we make our way to the bedroom. We didn't talk about much before we jumped into our Vegas wedding, but I'm pretty glad with how things worked out. We got lucky. I've never wanted kids, and he doesn't either. We've collected two cats over the past few years, but that's the most responsibility I'm willing to flesh out.

"How was work?"

I can't help but smile at the question, watching as he undresses at the foot of our bed. It's just funny to me how we can talk about mundane things like this as we get ready to fuck.

He's wearing a tight pair of red briefs, giving me a hint of nostalgia. We've been out of apartment thirteen for a couple of years, but sometimes I get glimpses of him, and it reminds me of our room there. Where we fought and fell in love.

"Work was work." Family counseling can be exhausting, but sometimes I get to genuinely help, and it makes those tough days worth it. I see a lot of myself in the kids I talk to, and maybe even understand things with my mom and dad a little better. Today was one of those good days, but coming home to my husband was definitely the best part.

Except we need to be done talking about work.

I place my hand on his throat, just a touch—so familiar by now—and smile at the need in his eyes.

BRIANNA FLORES

"On your knees, little brother."

Afterword

Woof. I cannot believe I actually managed to write this book. I want to say a big ol' thank you again to everyone who patiently (or not-so-patiently) waited for Cade's story. I know I wasn't a very active author on social media during the writing process, but to everyone who reached out and told me how excited you were for this book, I adore you!

I do want to let you know that though I am still not going to be very present on my socials, I am so, so grateful for any and all reviews. Feel free to leave them on Amazon or Goodreads, Instagram or wherever! I appreciate every review I get and they really do help so much when it comes to little indie authors like myself.

I *of course* have to give a thanks to the amazing community within the MM Book Rec group on Facebook. The interactions I have on that page keep me going, even if I'm not there as much as I used to be. You can always leave a review there-I promise I'll see it.

You're probably sick of my gratitude, but again, thank you!

-Brianna Flores

Books In This Series

The Boys of Apartment 13

The boys of apartment 13 are unlucky in love. From confusing bi-awakenings to unrequited feelings for your bestie, from the worst stepbrother you could ask for to craving the most annoying straight boy you've ever met, these boys just can't catch a break!

In this series, you'll find high-heat love stories with varying levels of angst that end happily ever after.

Each book can be read as a standalone, though the series may be better enjoyed if read in order!

Pretty Boy

Liam Walker doesn't get the hype surrounding sex. Not until he meets his ex-girlfriend's brother, that is. Suddenly, he's being treated like the princess he is, and he can't get enough!

Lover Boy

Good Boy

Francis "Baby" Holbrook has been frustrated (the sexual kind) ever since straight boy Logan Matthews moved in. Protecting his heart means not letting himself fall for Logan, and luckily, he's annoying enough that he makes it pretty easy.

But throw a little bondage and a lotta praise at Baby, and suddenly, it becomes a lot harder.

Lonely Boy

More info to come...

Printed in Great Britain
by Amazon

48578596R00161